5-
1st US
89

CRISSCROSS

CRISSCROSS

PAT FLOWER

STEIN AND DAY/*Publishers*/New York

First published in the United States of America, 1977
Copyright © 1976 by Pat Flower
All rights reserved
Printed in the United States of America
Stein and Day/*Publishers*/Scarborough House,
Briarcliff Manor, N.Y. 10510
ISBN 0-8128-2415-6

CHAPTER I

Edward counted ten ashtrays. One more than last time. All were big and deep, their rims overlapping the bowls so the ash wouldn't blow about. Some were round, some square. None was oblong, Sibyl didn't like oblongs. Most were seconds, gone a bit wonky during the throwing; not worth selling for the giveaway price they'd bring. If there must be ashtrays at all, Edward preferred these asymmetrical throw-outs. All were disgusting, crammed full of ash, butts, bits of screwed-up cellophane, olive stones, bits of biscuit gooey with dip. Some were a greeny-grey and some brownish, depending on where the clay came from. Sibyl liked them big for all the people who came, and also because they gave her a better chance of scoring a hit as she rushed about with a cigarette. She had ashtrays all over the house, not just this room. She liked them half-glazed and half-not, she'd been doing that a lot lately on everything. A transparent glaze you could see the clay through. These were all pretty recent; ashtrays and vases and stuff like that got broken a lot when meetings got excited. Sometimes she scratched whirly lines in the clay.

He thought a squarish green one was the newest, making ten. Sibyl would have brought it in from the pottery since Saturday, because it was after Saturday's meeting he'd counted nine.

Tonight's meeting had been the usual thing. Shouting, savouries, drinks, smoking, inconclusive. Somebody delegated to write a letter or seek an interview or organize a demo. What had it been about? Edward had heard 'elderly citizens' more than once, but that didn't prove anything. Land rezoning, sewerage, the blacks, pensions, inflation — there were a million things elderly citizens could be embroiled in. Or even old people, he thought with a smile. It was lucky he could shut his ears, even right in the thick of it. How Sibyl loved it all: calling meetings, organizing action, implementing resolutions in between her potting. It was both nourishment and drug to Sibyl.

Out in the kitchen, cleaning the ashtrays, Edward remembered Lindsay and felt the lilt again. If the thing with Lindsay came to anything Sibyl might have to curb her activities, or at any rate cut down the number of meetings held here in the house. If he collaborated with Lindsay — and Lindsay wouldn't have mentioned the project without something of the sort in mind — Edward would need a bit more peace and quiet to concentrate in. There was that big room upstairs that got the afternoon sun. It looked out over some waste ground beyond their own, and in the distance a housing development growing at snail's pace. Probably the room where noise penetrated least.

He saw Sibyl had scraped the dishes and stacked them with those from dinner. She'd be in bed by now.

He took the ashtrays back and ranged them carefully on the mantelpiece between Mummy's vases. Then he got the vacuum cleaner from under the stairs in the hall. But before starting he gathered and shook the millions of cushions and piled them in an armchair. All the cushions had frills, some had tassels, and even the three-piece lounge suite and two extra armchairs had loose covers Edward thought frilly. A pale pink curtain of flimsy stuff lunged suddenly inward at the open window. First breath of wind all evening. It stirred an ancient musty smell of dust and ashes. The flimsy curtains had frills sewn down all their sides and the heavier curtains which were sometimes pulled at night had their own stiff frills all round, even along the top where they hung on big wooden rings from a fat wooden rod. Edward knew all about the frills, the reasoning behind them. The silk lampshades were frilly too, their faded bright lolly pink almost matching, in daylight, that of the heavier curtains. At night like now all colour was swamped in the terrible glow of Sibyl's red and orange light bulbs.

With his hands he brushed crumbs, ash and other litter off the furniture, feeling down in the creases from old experience. His fingers encountered a bit of sardine and distaste twisted his face. He went to the window and threw it out past the curtain; one of the cats would find it.

He was to see Lindsay again on Friday. So far they'd only skirted the idea. Lindsay was coming up to the office after hours. It was decent of Lindsay to show him the ropes. Edward already had an angle Lindsay hadn't thought of. It wasn't too wildly improbable that Lindsay might find Edward indispensable. When fools rushed in it sometimes worked out better than angels. In any case, Edward wouldn't rush, he wasn't a rusher, he was far too timid. Lindsay knew how timid he was but at the same time Lindsay knew his value. Supposing it came off? The thought of it was so heady he felt limp. He wouldn't breathe a word to Sibyl unless it did, or until. God, wouldn't that make her sit up.

He plugged in the vacuum cleaner, switched it on and started on the rugs. You couldn't do rugs properly, they needed a good whacking outside. They all had enormous flowers on and masses of fringe and were dropped about on the wall-to-wall nylon carpet in a nutmeggy colour that didn't show the dirt. If Edward ever again had a room of his own it would be stark, functional, muted, and above all clean. He pictured the room upstairs.

He'd known Lindsay about seven years. It was through knowing Lindsay he'd met Sibyl, because he'd never have gone to see a play alone and he had nobody else to go with. What fragile things life hinged upon, he'd discovered. With a life so mapped out as his had been he'd given no thought to fragile hinges until Lindsay happened. Meeting Lindsay was a fragile hinge in itself, or rather Lindsay's taxation problems were the real hinge. Lindsay's tax had changed his life magically, and it looked as though the magic was still working.

He threw the rugs aside in a heap, one by one, and started on the carpet.

Lindsay was a scriptwriter – well, a writer whose main work was television scripts. He'd done a few films for the government crowd. He also wrote magazine stuff plus other odds and ends. He knew everyone worth knowing in his field. The new project was a film about ecology. Australian. Roughly an hour, Lindsay thought. Edward suspected Lindsay might not know the real meaning of ecology. It was a fashionable word. Lindsay threw it around with as little feeling as he'd thrown around other trendy words until something new came along. Still, he was an experienced writer. He'd been strangely vague today for an experienced writer. No hook to hang it on. He'd talked about shooting from a plane, a helicopter and ground vehicles. What about on foot? Edward had thought.

'We'll rope in expert opinion, old boy, of course,' Lindsay had said, 'so what d'you think, d'you like the general idea?'

Edward said he did. He didn't go overboard because Lindsay had his sideways sardonic little smile.

'Toss it around,' Lindsay had said carelessly. 'I'd like your views.'

No wonder Edward felt the lilt. He hadn't been so excited since the first days of Sibyl. This was a more exciting excitement. Lindsay wanted his views. A successful creative person wanted Edward's views. What could be headier? Edward could feel views stirring and taking shape. He remembered Sibyl saying once, after one of her environment meetings, 'Every teeniest thing has a life of its own, every plant and ant and caterpillar, they *all* count, darling, and they're all *interdependent*.' Sibyl's teeny things made planes and helicopters look a bit silly.

He put all the ashtrays back in the exact places they'd been in before.

So Edward felt he knew a bit more, in fact a whole lot more, about the subject than Lindsay did. Edward had picked up a lot from Sibyl, not just the names of big issues like Lake Pedder and Myall Lakes and rain forests and the crown of thorns, but all sorts of subsidiary and even detailed stuff about forests and water tables and a million things he could ask Sibyl about. Didn't she have a whole lot of stuff in pamphlets and minutes? Lindsay's approach was stereotyped. He'd do his research, of course, but where was the vision, the spark? Even an experienced writer should glow at the start of things. Lindsay was too used to rattling things off. Most of his work was commissioned. This was different. Lindsay had said nothing about any backing so it was off the top of his head. Lindsay was boastful, and if this film were anything more than a shot in the dark he wouldn't be able to resist saying so. He was always on about his commissions and useful contacts, he dropped names in the same casual way he dropped his cigarette ash.

While he was winding the vacuum's flex Sibyl came in. She was in cold cream and her robe.

'You're an absolute *angel*, Eddie darling.'

He pulled a funny frowning face.

'*Edward* darling,' she corrected.

Edward went out with the vacuum cleaner. When he came back Sibyl had shut the window and pulled the heavy curtains across. Edward went to the heap of rugs. He knew exactly where each went because of the order he'd piled them in. He heard Sibyl's lighter.

Had Lindsay thought of a name? They'd need what Lindsay called a working title. *Wheels Across the Outback* flashed through Edward's mind. It had the sort of hackneyed sound Lindsay might come up with.

'What's funny, sugar?' Sibyl said.

'Just something happened in the office.' Would he ever get Sibyl to stop calling him sugar? Perhaps when his name was among the credits up on the screen.

'It must have been a scream, whatever it was.' She flopped into one of the armchairs and flicked her ash at the second-nearest ashtray.

Edward finished plumping the dreadful cushions. He put one at Sibyl's back. 'I'll do the washing-up now.' He wanted to kiss her hair but the cold cream put him off.

'I've *done* it, darling nitwit. Didn't you hear it panting? It's just about finished.'

Edward looked at the room. Was that everything? He went to the mantelpiece and moved the left-hand vase an inch to the right.

Sibyl laughed. 'When Mummy dies I'll chuck them out. She knows it's you takes all the loving care.'

Edward hated the vases, big ugly twins sploshed with some supposed folk art pattern native to somewhere in Europe.

'You're an *angel* the way you always clean up after.' Sibyl sighed. 'Coming to bed?'

'Any minute now.' *Heritage and Outrage,* he thought. *Vanished Dreamtime. The Big Gamble* – no, that sounded like an old movie. He'd like to come up with a working title that would make Lindsay's eyes pop open.

And Sibyl's. He smiled at her. 'I hoped it wasn't cold cream night.'

'Oh *gosh.*' She knew what he meant. 'I'll get rid of it, darling. You know me and my poor old face, it's just when I happen to *remember* it.' She got up and stubbed out the cigarette. 'Don't be long.'

After she'd gone Edward got a couple of tissues from the box in the sideboard and cleaned the ashtray she'd used. Then he did the rounds of locks and bolts, made sure in the kitchen that Sibyl had lodged the dishwasher open, and went upstairs. It felt even hotter upstairs. Hot air rises. It was an old house, but not old enough to be cool with thick stone walls. Just old enough for its bricks to hold the heat. The advantage of high ceilings was dissipated by the hot inland suburb they lived in.

The bedroom light was off. Sibyl was waiting for him in the dark. Her eyes would be open, he knew. He was glad she wasn't smoking. Edward undressed in the dark and went along the passage to the bathroom. One of the improvements he'd wanted was a modern bathroom connected to their bedroom. He always felt somehow sneaky leaving the bedroom to go to the bathroom and then creeping back, like a funny man in a bedroom farce invading the wrong room.

The tepid shower was nice. The winter months of June, July and August hadn't been cold, never crisp. The whole year waterlogged with rain. It was much the same now in October, just warmer. As humid, day after day of rain, floods occurring in parts of the country that never had them before, or not for umpteen years. Today in Sydney it had eased a bit and tonight's breath of wind might augur a change. What was it doing ecologically? Could a year of rain affect an immemorial process? Speed it up or slow it down? But shifts in weather were themselves part of the process, weren't they? They weren't imposed from outside the relationship like the things science was doing: man's barbaric encroachments. Yet hadn't he read somewhere they were doing exactly that: developing a weapon able to change weather, impose at will its worst manifestations? Would Lindsay pose such questions? Edward thought not.

When he slipped into Sibyl's bed her arms enfolded him. What a darling she was. A bit clammy, but who wasn't in this weather? No trace of the cold cream. Their kiss was long and deep and swoony. It was marvellous the way after six whole years, a bit more, she still shivered at his caresses.

Marvellous too that he wasn't shy with Sibyl. Of course after six years – but Edward was sure that with any other woman he'd always have felt constraint. Not that there'd have been any other woman. He'd have hung back as always. It was only because of the way they'd met, with Lindsay and Diana on hand to make it in a way inevitable. Plus some magic of Sibyl's. Even so he'd been wary at the rather leathery skin she had these sudden bursts of that. Forget deficiencies. Everything had been natural because Sibyl made it so. It had been in his flat at Elizabeth Bay, that first time. And the other times until they married. Never at her Forest Lodge place. He'd thought then it was because she shared it with Diana.

Even in the dark where he couldn't see its colour he could see the chestnut of her hair. And her freckles. And the rather leathery skin she had these sudden bursts of cold cream about. And her darlingness in loving him and still wanting his love. He was practised now.

Sibyl smothered his face and neck with little nibbly kisses. *Deathly Union. Union of Death.* No, rotten. Something would come to him.

She'd been so easy to get along with. It had been a first such experience for Edward, even including Lindsay, because Lindsay's friendships were admittedly based upon what he could get out of them. Lindsay's palliness gave Edward a shamed feeling. Lindsay could find another tax accountant, but why go to all that trouble when there was Edward? Edward wished he could breeze through life like Lindsay.

But what was in it for Sibyl? There'd be a million men she could choose from.

She was asleep. The deep ratchety breathing caught now and then in her throat. Her lungs must be jet-black with all the smoking. He gave her hair a gossamer kiss, eased away from the hand on his chest and then from her bed.

His own felt cool and clean.

They'd met during the interval of some play he couldn't remember. Edward went with Lindsay who said it was an allegory and trod on the foot of the girl Sibyl was with. Lindsay and the dark girl hit it off at once. Her name was Diana Lucas. Edward felt her instant dislike. Sibyl was Sibyl Finch and she smiled at Edward while Lindsay fell all over Diana. Sibyl's hair was chestnut. He'd never seen a chestnut but he knew the colour. Light blue eyes, lots of laughter lines. Not too tall, a nice height, thinnish. Diana and Lindsay were talking about the play, Lindsay with his air of knowing criticizing its construction. Edward asked Sibyl did she write. She said with a laugh, 'I pot a bit.' She shared a flat with Diana at Forest Lodge. Edward said he was at Elizazeth Bay. 'Within striking distance,' she laughed. She laughed a lot. It had been instantaneous. A bond he knew was permanent just in the interval of a play. He went home on a cloud, scarcely listening to Lindsay's appreciative dissection of Diana. Only one thing penetrated: Lindsay had got Diana's phone number. It would be Sibyl's too. There'd been two days and nights of agony wrestling with his cold feet, wondering if her 'striking distance' had been a real invitation. Then Edward got the number from Lindsay and dared to telephone. Blissfully Sibyl was there, blissfully delighted to hear from him. After that it was plain sailing. He felt at home with her. She was so happy, she laughed and made him laugh. He didn't have to make an effort, she took their being together for granted, she understood. He was able to talk without fear of boring her, he was able to tell her his ambition to be a writer. He chose writing because of Lindsay and because they'd met at a play, and because Sibyl wasn't a writer. But the truth was Edward yearned for any creative outlet. He told her he could never seem to find the time to get started. She understood and sympathized. Miles better than his mother, the antithesis. It was great, it was a miracle.

He felt himself drifting into sleep. *The Living Wilderness. Wilderness Alive. Links in a Chain.* Links, links – he lost the thread, nearly asleep. *Broken Links.* Links what? His mind tried to grapple. Cufflinks? He fell asleep with golf links.

CHAPTER II

Edward was waiting for Lindsay. Mr Strachan, the senior partner, had been the last to go. He'd popped a warm smile in and said, 'Don't overdo it, Mr Piper, have a nice week-end,' and then had gone thin and tall in his stuffy hat and the briefcase that was always tucked under his left arm.

Edward cleared his desk to the efficient bareness Mr Strachan's always had. Then he got up and went along the corridor to the door marked MEN. Drying his hands he looked in the glass and was struck by how little he'd aged in the last ten years. Changing his job had been the start of it, the first self-initiated move, the first courageous step. It had brought him Lindsay, then a year later Sibyl. In his seventh year of marriage he looked as young as on their wedding day. At thirty-six he looked in his late twenties. Small features, small ears, good teeth, all things neat and even. He took care of himself, jog-trotting every week-end and sometimes evenings. Fair crinkly hair sat close to his head with little curls at the tips. His voice was mild, his manner gentle. He guessed Lindsay thought him a dope. But Edward knew the strength of his thick-set body and revelled in it. He wasn't exactly tall but he was taller than Lindsay. Lindsay was weedy; Edward could flatten him in seconds if he wanted to. The idea made him smile. Then his eyes – Sibyl was crazy about his eyes, a deeper blue than hers and deep-set. 'Such *mysterious pools,* darling,' Sybil said.

He went back to the office. Lindsay should be here by now. He'd have some easy excuse, an apology his crooked smile would nullify. Edward felt a twinge of annoyance; after all, Lindsay had done the broaching. Another thing that annoyed him was he couldn't remember any of the titles he'd thought of. He should have jotted them down. Lindsay jotted everything down. A couple had been downright brilliant.

It seemed all at once dark. Edward looked round at the sky through his tenth-floor window and saw the clouds were back, massed and threatening. At any rate the traffic would have thinned a bit by the time he left for the long drive home. He had a blank pad and a pencil but nothing came. He'd hoped to score at the outset with a perfect title. Lindsay was probably drinking somewhere, he drank a lot. Sometimes his small hazel eyes nearly disappeared in the to look at: short, ears a bit pointed, gingery sideburns, red sore rims he got from drinking, and his wispy, longish, light brown hair looked wispier. Lindsay wasn't much tiny red eyes. A bachelor, thought himself a sexpot; always boasting about the girls he was on with. He still saw Diana Lucas, so Diana must be worth-while in that department. It was none of Edward's business.

Edward was secretly ashamed for Lindsay yet grateful for his friendship. When Sibyl disparaged him Edward said nothing. Sibyl didn't trust Lindsay, she said he was meretricious and would sell out every principle for a turn of phrase. No one was faultless, Edward thought; hadn't Sibyl heard about beams and motes?

Lindsay breezed in with a knock and a stagger and the gnomish tilted smile. 'Sorry I'm late, old boy, script conference.'

'It's all right,' Edward smiled. At that moment it struck him that Lindsay's drinking and sardonic humour might be the mask for a sense of inferiority. Lindsay poked too much fun at far too many things. 'You going to sit down?'

Lindsay looked at the chair opposite Edward and threw his bulging old briefcase on it. Then he perched on the desk. 'Christ, what a day! – that bloody Sutton, mind of a louse, you don't know how bloody lucky you are.' He looked at the quiet of the office with a face of envy.

Edward smiled his tolerant smile.

'Well, how's it shaping?' Lindsay said. He lit a cigarette. 'Done any thinking?'

'Some.' That was a Lindsay usage and Edward enjoyed saying it. 'I've thought of a working title for a start.' It had just come into his head.

'Good. Let's hear it.'

'*Living Union.*'

Lindsay stared, then laughed so that he couldn't speak. Edward watched him. He'd never felt angry with Lindsay before but he'd never been laughed at by Lindsay before. It didn't seem all that hilarious. Lindsay looked quite horrible, shoulders hunched and his straggly hair sticking over his collar. And his eyes watering. At last he managed to splutter, '*Living Union,*' then a fresh paroxysm started. Then at last he said, 'Christ, no offence, old boy, sounds like a bloody trade union undefunct.'

Edward smiled. 'Now you mention it, yes. It's only one of a few I've been tossing around.' He liked saying tossing around, too.

'The title's no worry,' Lindsay said, 'premature at this stage unless it's bang-on. It'll come in the process. Matter of fact I've got a working title.'

'Oh, I see.' Edward waited.

'*Here is my Space,*' Lindsay said without a trace of embarrassment. 'Like it?'

It was Edward's turn to stare. He would have liked to laugh as Lindsay had laughed. He thought the title pretentious and silly. Irrelevant, too. He kept his face judicious and made no comment.

'It's from *Antony and Cleo*, 1.1.33.' Lindsay grinned through his smoke. 'Of course old Cleo wasn't speaking ecologically, but it seems to fit, nice possessive ring to it – *our* country, *my* space – sort of thing.'

Edward said it was very good.

'The main thing is the approach,' Lindsay said.

'I'd have thought the first thing,' Edward said.

Lindsay gave him a sharp unsmiling look. After a thoughtful moment he said, 'Well, any ideas?'

'Yes. You said about planes and helicopters and surface vehicles. I got the picture of vast tracts without any detailed study of what happens. I mean the interaction between climate and plant, plant and animal and insect, wind and water and what man's doing, mining and pollution. Everything has its own life but all life is interdependent.'

There was no derisive laughter. 'Well, you've done some bloody thinking all right, but that sort of watchful study could take years.'

'Why not?' Edward said.

'Not practicable, old boy.'

'Why not?'

'Well – ' Lindsay hesitated, then the grin came. 'Backing, for one thing, never get the backing for such a long-drawn-out project.'

'Why not?'

'You sound like a broken record, old boy. I'll tell you why not. Backing's bloody impossible to get these days anyway, bloody tight money, costs shot up and the rest of it. Backers want returns pronto, quick profits, even the bloody government crowd. Quick returns, quick shooting – your kind of long loving look the cost'd be bloody astronomical.'

'What about the conservation people?'

Lindsay did a humourless mocking laugh and said, 'Don't

make me laugh, poor as bloody church mice.'

Edward drew a tree on his pad. 'Isn't the project hopeless from the start then?'

Lindsay gave him another look. He stubbed his cigarette in Edward's clean glass ashtray. Then he said, 'It's worth a go. No skin off our noses if it doesn't come off. Training for you and I'm sitting pretty anyway. Half the battle's getting the thing on paper, all worked out. You've got a commodity for sale.'

'Yes, I see.' Edward was making it a leafy tree. 'I still think your way's hackneyed. *Wheels Across the Outback.*' It had just come back to him.

'Who said anything about – look, that stuff was off the top of my head, something to kick around. I like your detailed thing so long as the shooting's quick.'

'The commentary could handle the time element, the slow process,' Edward said. 'Deft, of course, nothing cumbersome.'

'Might work.' Lindsay looked dubious. He slid from the desk and walked about the office. 'The last thing we want is a great wordy lecture.'

Edward saw the words as sparse, as a brief explanatory back-up only where needed. He'd seen a few good documentaries. But he said nothing. He drew fresh bunches of bipinnate leaves.

Lindsay said, 'For what it's worth, how about Sibyl? She might be good for a few lurks.'

There was no doubt Lindsay thought of everything. Edward had meant to keep Sibyl up his sleeve. 'Yes, she's fairly up in this sort of thing, knows a few people, but I'd say direct research would be better scriptwise.' It made him feel professional saying scriptwise.

'Sound her out, old boy,' Lindsay said carelessly. He lugged his briefcase up from the chair and plonked it on the desk. 'Let's make that today's little project.' He looked bored and ready to go.

'What about the approach?' Edward said. He drew three neat horizontal lines under the tree.

'No worries,' Lindsay said, 'the stuff we come up with'll give us the approach, same as the title.'

'Okay.' But Edward didn't agree.

'Well, cheers, old boy, you coming now?'

'Pee first.'

'Me too.'

They parted out on the street. The homegoing traffic had thinned a lot. Edward went to the parking station where he was a permanent client.

Lindsay was coming up to the office again on Monday. A whole week-end to think in. Edward hoped Sibyl hadn't got crowds coming. Usually she forgot to tell him, yet her genuine remorse never seemed to prevent the next lapse into thoughtlessness. He'd have to cut down the jog-trots now he was working with Lindsay. That wouldn't matter: it was mental exercise he craved. Physically he was in the pink. Creative stimulus, to be thinking creatively.

Even the run of red lights didn't worry him.

He looked forward to long sessions of creative inter-change. Excitement caught his throat. Why, already today he'd found courage to say things he hadn't dreamed he could ever say. It was stimulating to talk *with* Lindsay instead of being talked *at*. Promoted from being Lindsay's sounding-board. Even to challenge Lindsay – there'd been a couple of times Lindsay looked at him as though he really had something to contribute, a different outlook. Slant, Lindsay would call it.

He got the lights with him when he turned on to Route 31. He was used now to the long drive morning and evening. The dismay, the resentment, he'd felt when Sibyl sprang the house on him had dulled into the acceptance he accorded all things. Just before their wedding. A scattering of houses and filling stations called Fernydale, outside Liverpool, not even on the map, with neither fern nor dale.

Funny the way one adapted to anathemas. It was just a
nuisance it was so far from town. Lindsay had a big, expensive, creative-looking unit on the harbour at Double
Bay, and Edward would feel surer about the collaboration
if he lived close by. You couldn't dash 33 kilometres late
at night say, and stay agog with some new arguable angle.
The telephone wasn't the same, you missed nuances.

Lindsay was four years younger and looked as much
older. Strange Lindsay should think of Sibyl; Lindsay and
Sibyl hadn't met more than a few times. He remembered
his theory of Lindsay's inferiority. A lot pointed to it. His
language, for instance : all the Christs and bloodys. His
attitude to women : wasn't that called a basic insecurity?
And treating so lightly Edward's ideas after seeking his
help. Wasn't it likely Lindsay would jot them down, was
probably doing so now in the nearest bar? Lindsay was
always on the make, boasted of it. On the subject of
inferiority Edward felt himself a specialist. He thought
Lindsay might brag and blaspheme, even cheat, under a
stress that would send Edward further into his shell. In
any case Edward would learn from the experience, and he
was the one had access to any titbits from Sibyl.

Lindsay looked not much different now from when
Edward first met him, seven to eight years ago. He'd looked
worn even then, sort of seedy. Already successful at twenty-
four. The same range of sardonic comment, updated now
only by topical allusion. But he'd opened up Edward's
life and Edward still felt the warm gratitude and friendship he'd felt then. It took courage, but he even telephoned
Lindsay sometimes, though never without good reason :
had Lindsay seen some play that was in the news, or
Edward had read a rave review of a TV play by somebody
else, or maybe a variation in taxation that might or might
not affect Lindsay, or would Lindsay care to hear an idea
Edward had for a series? Lindsay had sometimes sounded
interrupted but the telephone interrupted everyone, didn't

it? Edward was sure he'd never shown the envy of Lindsay he felt. Lindsay was the closest thing to a friend Edward ever had.

Life for Edward had been so dull he scarcely remembered his childhood. Just a succession of days and years and his father dying. Killed in the war the year it ended, when Edward was five. His mother battling, that was his chief memory. She spoke of it daily. He sensed that her loss and grief were far worse than he could know about. He was always conscious, much more than his older sister Alice was, of their mother's efforts to bring them up 'nicely'. The care and sacrifice. He'd been especially protective, pandering to whims and moods that otherwise might have been trying.

At school shyness had kept him out of groups. Other boys flung themselves outwards, and if their bravado was sometimes misplaced they could laugh it off and hurl themselves against the next test. Edward was full of self-doubts that made him timid and awkward. He was no good at games despite his burly build. It was a mental attitude that fed on itself. Yet the more he hung back, the more certain he was of some specialness inside him.

But there was always the persistent, distracting need to do well academically to please his mother. He'd studied hard, with results that gratified her. She pushed him into university where he did two-thirds of an arts course, then got him a job she couldn't let slip by. It was with a firm of accountants, one of whose presiding partners was her solicitor's cousin. Edward had done a book-keeping course before university, at a business college, discovering an aptitude. When his mother's move switched him back to figures Edward didn't say I told you so. His mother tried her best.

Big drops splashed on the windscreen and then it was a fury, hurled by the wind. Edward hoped Sibyl would watch his herbs.

The job was safe and dull. His contact with people was small and restricted to their financial affairs. He longed for some artistic outlet, felt himself on its brink. But what brink? How recognize it? Inside him were bottled painter, sculptor, novelist, poet, along with the self-distrust which imprisoned them. Irresolution increased his timidity, he hung back from meeting people. It was a lonely life. When Alice married and moved to Perth, a continent away, Edward felt more than ever trapped. Alice had escaped, he was stuck with his mother. And lonelier. It didn't help that he knew this to be unreasonable, an excuse for his own failure to act. Four years later when his mother moved to Perth to help Alice bring up her children, she did it knowing Edward was safe for life. He felt discarded, somehow manipulated, and the hurt of it made him remember her interferences. With more adult and objective guidance, he thought, he'd have had a different career, a creative career; he might have lost his shyness, he might have got to know girls, felt at ease with them, picked and chosen. It was sheer luck a darling like Sibyl had been the first girl to notice him.

He was twenty-seven at the time of his mother's defection. He was on his own. He knew it was now or never before bitterness and apathy engulfed him. There was nobody to ask or answer to. He had to do something or stay for ever smothered. Others did exciting flamboyant things, even dangerous things. They took risks. He read about them in newspapers. There was always somebody somewhere having a ball over something. The impulse won and Edward broke out of his job and into another. Exhilaration was intense but brief. What he'd found with impeccable references was another accounting firm. It was a frying-pan-to-fire move. It seemed a worse deadendery. Edward was at his lowest ebb. Until, two years later, he met Lindsay Reid and Lindsay's taxation problems.

Edward's firm specialized in taxation.

Lindsay opened a door on the world Edward longed for. He threw himself into Lindsay's tax as if it were his first poem. Lindsay's tax put Edward on the fringe of litera- ture. He found loopholes and dodges that were all legal. He was able to make legitimate deductions Lindsay had never heard of. In Lindsay's eyes Edward was tops, but it was Lindsay who was the creator. When the relationship lasted, branched out beyond the office, Edward told him- self friendships grew out of slighter things and was grate- ful. Lindsay was casual the way Edward would like to be. Casual about girls, fitting them round and in between the important business of writing. Edward envied Lindsay his smile. But when he tried to imitate the sardonic twist in the glass at home it somehow wouldn't work, he had the wrong face. Lindsay's face was made for it.

Edward knew Sibyl was out before turning into their road. It was a feeling he got, invariably confirmed when her battered old station wagon was missing from the grass verge. Sibyl let Edward have the garage for his classier car.

The house glowed like a sunset through the rain. She always left all the lights on for burglars. There must be a meeting she'd forgotten to tell him about. The garage was at the back and he always went in that way. The long, coarse, unkempt grass the garden was full of was beaten flat by wind and rain. His herbs were all right, protected under the castor oil tree that had got too big against the house. She hadn't locked the back door. She was always in such a rush. Three complaining cats and Sibyl's coloured lights. The cats purred round his legs and wailed their grievances: hunger and the weather.

He got a gin and tonic and fed the cats. There seemed a lot of not done washing-up and nothing for dinner. Edward boiled himself two eggs and Sibyl came in just on the end of them. She stared in a pose of drama and dripped on the terracotta tiles.

'You said you were *out* for dinner, sugar.'

Edward smiled. 'I said I was meeting Lindsay, that's all. It's all right, eggs are fine.'

'*Gosh,* darling, I'm sorry.'

'You have a meeting?'

'Sort of, not that kind.' She stood her umbrella in the sink and hung her raincoat behind the kitchen door. 'Just with the Cliffords, early dinner because of the kids, Nance made a *dreadful* pie just like concrete.' She flung her arms round Edward from behind and kissed his hair. 'Darling, Jeff's so *enthusiastic,* he says all I need for a one-woman show is just to get *cracking.*'

'Good for Jeff.' Edward patted her hands.

She thrust her face round his and looked into his eyes. 'Would *you* buy one of my pots at an exhibition?'

He kissed her nose. 'If I had a use for one, of course, darling.'

'I can't think why I love you, you're such a *functional* man.'

After she'd gone upstairs he took her umbrella out into the hall and opened it to dry. Edward didn't like umbrellas in the sink.

CHAPTER III

Edward was down first on Saturday morning. Two cats sat by the kitchen door and watched in sullen silence. The third, hearing his footsteps, shot in through the cat door and rubbed wetly round his legs. Edward opened the back door. It was clammy against his hand. The depression he felt wasn't just the rain, it was a vague compound of everything. Thriving weeds, the sodden drive, the old brick outhouse with its blackened chimney Sibyl called her potshot, the cats, the week-end. Even Lindsay, even Sibyl's exhibition she was so excited about. He left the door open and went in the kitchen. He gave the cats their milk then washed his hands at the sink. He didn't like to wash his hands at the sink but the downstairs bathroom had the castor oil tree outside and he couldn't face its big, wet, stupid leaves sneering in at him. Sibyl wouldn't have it touched. There was also an outside loo where Edward had got a hand basin put in. He directed Sibyl's people either there or to the castor oil bathroom, although Sibyl didn't mind them trooping upstairs to their private bathroom.

He opened the kitchen window and the frilly curtain blew clammily against his face.

Sibyl felt like an egg, she said. Edward got out three and then set the table. Sibyl always liked one Weetabix with honey. There was no need for curtains, nobody overlooked them and there were blinds for night. He thought for the thousandth time how the gleaming modern equipment (even grubby it still gleamed) looked at odds in the big old kitchen. Dishwasher, stove, refrigerator, washing machine and lots of smaller appliances. Edward would have started from scratch and made the kitchen a totally modern well-functioning unit. Walls, ceiling and all. Just kept the quarry tiles on the floor and the big pine table. New windows, much bigger, no curtains.

Now that Sibyl must work hard for her show – and Jeff would insist – the house would be freer of people. Sibyl had been too generous with her time (and Edward's). Members of various organizations were too used to taking the house for granted as a meeting-place. Sibyl couldn't produce first-rate ceramics and still carry on in the same old way. So it coincided nicely with Lindsay's thing and Edward's need for a quiet working atmosphere. Good for Jeff.

Jeff Clifford was himself a successful potter, did a lot

of arty sculptural stuff, and praise from him meant a lot. Nice enough fellow, fortyish, impressive appearance: tall and spare, tanned face, white hair, black eyebrows, small, dark, lively eyes. Spoke little, too, a rare quality among, Sibyl's vociferous gang. The only thing Edward had against him was his pipe-smoking; part of the image, of course, but a disgusting habit all the same. His wife Nance was around the same age, short, fattish, friendly, cigarettes. Grey eyes, a mass of mousy hair pinned back anyhow. A dreadful cook and always at it, never arrived without some treat she'd just run up. On all the committees and two sons around nine and ten, yet Nance seemed somehow to muddle through.

He heard Sibyl coming down and switched the eggs and toast on. He heard the Weetabix rustle as he started the kettle.

'Nearly out of honey,' Sibyl said, 'oh *gosh*!'

'What's up?' He was watching the eggs.

'The week-end shopping, somehow it got away.'

'I'll do it,' Edward said.

'*Darling* you are.'

Sibyl always meant to get it done on Friday. A few times Edward had suggested deliveries but Sibyl liked to see what she was buying. Since the job fell mostly to Edward her objection about deliveries lost its point. It was one of those jokes families build up, Edward supposed.

Seated opposite her he said, 'Quiet week-end, I hope.'

'Only Sunday lunch,' Sibyl said, 'why, darling – tired?'

'Some work I want to get at.' Even just saying it quickened his pulse.

'Me too,' Sibyl said. 'Jeff's got me really hard at it.' Then she said, '*You* work – what at?'

He couldn't keep it in, it was too exciting; besides, he'd need all the help she could give him. 'An idea Lindsay's got for a film, wants me to help him with it.'

'Oh – *Lindsay*!'

'What's that mean?' Edward got up to make the tea.

'I just don't *trust* Lindsay.'

'That's irrational.'

'What's the film about?'

'Ecology in Australia.'

'*Aha!*'

Edward brought the teapot. 'That was fraught with something.'

'It's plain as a pikestaff – he wants to pump *me* through *you* – you'd pass it all on like the sweet trusting lamb you are and he'd *pinch* it, darling.'

It didn't occur to Sibyl that Lindsay wanted Edward's help for its own sake. But all he said was, 'Since you've steered clear of Lindsay how can you be so certain about his character?'

'Women just *know* about people.'

Edward smiled and let it go. The rain had stopped and there were pale gleams from the hidden sun.

While he was out shopping he wondered whether there might be another reason for Sibyl's attitude about the film. Like for instance envy. He liked the idea. It would make a nice change, because all along he'd secretly envied Sibyl her ceramics, the doing of something creative. Not the sort of cerebral something he wanted (Edward saw nothing cerebral in Sibyl's utility pots) but better than the nothing he'd achieved. If Sibyl's accusations were true and Lindsay's purpose was simply to milk Edward, then Edward would take good care it didn't happen. But the idea was nonsense. Sibyl was too used to the skulduggeries that went on in her committees. *Symbiosis or Disaster.* No, terrible, too high-flown. Besides, Lindsay was going to stick to *Here is my Space.* Lindsay thought himself a dab hand at titles.

Edward enjoyed Saturday shopping now that he knew the Liverpool shopkeepers. It had taken a long time to overcome his reserve, but he no longer felt singled out to

be stared at. They called him Mr Piper and always had
a cheery word about rising prices.

While Sibyl got lunch he poked around his herbs. Parsley yellowing a bit, rosemary dying, but mint and chives
flourishing. Thyme and sage healthy, but something with
a rain-sodden label was dead and Edward couldn't remember what it was. Marjoram, perhaps? All in all, not
bad going for an accountant with a genius for Lindsay's
taxation. He liked herbs for their neatness. They were like
orderly columns of figures. He could be meticulous with
herbs in their little beds. He could control them.

He turned then and looked at the overgrown wilderness
of grass and weeds. Gardening on that scale didn't attract
him and it was easy to find he had no time for it. He'd
seen neighbours caught in its week-end bind. In the six
years since their wedding houses had sprung up and the
males, sweaty in shorts, dug and planted and hoed and
mowed and washed their cars all week-end long. The
Pipers' wasteland lowered the tone, their faces said. Sometimes Sibyl stuffed in quick growers donated by friends and
at once forgot them, so they straggled and died and joined
the mess of weeds. Not even a decent tree, just a few old
eucalypti down one side.

The afternoon jangled with telephone calls. Edward
kept hoping one might be Lindsay with a thought to toss
around. But they were all for Sibyl and he heard her voice
going on and on about starting or stopping something or
saving something else. Edward found he couldn't think,
even upstairs shut in the bare room he still seemed to hear
her public-spirited voice with all its indignations underlined. There was a Moreton Bay fig they were bent on
saving. It was funny to look out on their own desolate
ground and hear Sibyl saving public trees. Edward admired her selfless devotion to worthy causes. Old buildings,
the blacks, pensioners, urban environment, pollution, spas-
tics, abortion, divorce, uranium, supersonic aircraft, unwed

mothers, world famine. She talked in knowing detail on everything from human priorities to manufacturers labels, and went on deputations to rail against men in authority. He admired it while he felt it grow intolerable. It swamped his free time, his privacy, his life. Often he had to get his own dinner. Sibyl knew every brick and timber and paving stone in Liverpool, but to Edward it was just a place of buildings and streets they lived just out of.

He stood in the bare room. This would be the solution, with Lindsay's thing. It was nearly five, too late to start any housework. There wasn't an ecological thought in his head. He could go for a jog-trot in the mud. He went to the window. The rain was starting. The front garden was much smaller than the back, and equally uncared-for. The back of the house served in essence as the front. The road was better, there was more sun, the drive was there with all its comings and goings, the garage, Sibyl's kiln, the barbecue set among wild grass which Sibyl, but usually Edward, beat down for outdoor conviviality.

Tomorrow morning he'd get down to Lindsay's thing, make an early start.

During dinner, a sort of stew with a lot of the yellowing parsley in it, he said he'd use the upstairs room at the front to work in.

'But it's *bare,* darling.'

'That's what I like about it.'

Sibyl said he could have that little table which was always in the way in the upstairs hall. 'You're only going to write, aren't you?'

They settled on an old dining chair Sibyl had in the living-room in case anyone brought along someone extra, and which she hated.

'Hope the phone keeps quiet this evening,' Edward said.

'I've unplugged it, sugar, I'm going to think out the exhibition and make notes.'

Edward took the chair upstairs and placed it with the

table against one wall. Then he got a notepad and pencil and shut himself in. The naked light bulb dead centre shone in his eyes. He tried the table sideways but the irritating light insinuated its glare. He'd keep the white walls, just somehow organize the lighting. Clever indirect stuff, unobtrusive. He turned facing the wall with his back to the light.

The quiet was intense. Just beating rain. Had Sibyl left the dishes? He drew a row of beetles on his notepad. Then he made a border of them all round. He drew a tree in the middle. His mind was empty. Once the room was right – atmosphere was just as important as privacy and silence. He'd do it himself, just go right ahead and get it done. Bare simplicity, it shouldn't take long.

He should have done that with the house, just gone ahead. Only a few improvements, all much cheaper then. But Sibyl had said leave it to her. And the house had been only one shock among several. The shocks seemed trivial now, the important thing was *they* had survived.

He'd been so immensely in love. Sibyl too. Making him laugh. He wasn't an easy laugher. Giving him a sense of his own worth. When he deprecated his job she said, 'You'd have to be absolutely *brilliant* to get it and hold it, so think how they must *appreciate* you.' He wasn't really a junior partner but it was only the tiny lie of a man's vanity. She was good for his ego on all counts. Always eager to make love. Stayed overnight in his flat any time he wanted. He dreaded the thought that it might end, that she'd tire of him. He couldn't lose her. Couldn't face loneliness again. In a burst of desperate courage he'd mentioned marriage and Sibyl had laughed, not at him but at marriage. She said there was no better way to kill love stone dead. Edward agreed, feeling daring, remembering his mother. They'd live together, Sibyl said it would be much more fun. Edward thought a nice modern unit all built-ins. But Sibyl couldn't bear the pollutions of inner-city noise and fumes. 'Somewhere out of town but in *touch*, darling, you'll be so much healthier.' Edward was in great shape; only losing Sibyl could damage his health.

They'd considered where, jumping all over the map, then somehow it had finished with Sibyl's choice. They'd gone to the Liverpool area, looked at land blocks. His own land, his own house, putting down roots! Then Sibyl had said, 'Come and see a lovely old house, darling, you'll *adore* it.' They went to see it. It even had a kiln in a brick outhouse, but that had to wait for hindsight and by then it was too late.

Edward found he had no more room for the pattern of stylized flowers crammed between the tree and the border of beetles. He started a new page.

In those days he was in euphoria land. They went inside, and Edward didn't even question how: Sibyl at that time held the key to everything. He followed her over the house. He loved her hair and his eyes on it, following. The house was a mess though, he'd noticed that. Looked lived-in by a prize slouch. It was Victorian with high ceilings, three rooms and a bathroom upstairs, and downstairs a living-room, dining-room, the big kitchen, a pantry and another bathroom, and attached outside an unused laundry stuffed with junk and a loo. Sash windows with enormous sills, solid doors; it was all solid and all rundown. Some massive old furniture, masses of chintzy frills.

'You really like it?' Edward said.

'Well, isn't it *perfect, Eddie*?'

'Who lives here?'

'It's *available*, darling.'

'It'd need a thorough clean before I could move in. New furniture, the works. Did the occupants die suddenly?'

Sibyl laughed. 'It's only dust.'

He'd been a pushover. He'd had to learn later about Sibyl's clutter.

'Suppose they come back and catch us?' he said.

Sibyl was tickled pink. 'It's a *surprise*, darling,' she said, '*I* live here.'

Then the explanation: she'd been staying with Diana Lucas in the Forest Lodge flat only because Diana had just moved away from home and felt a bit lonely. Some such thing. And she'd wanted him to like the district and fall in love with the house. Which he hadn't. But he'd smiled and gone along and felt only a momentary suffocation, because Sibyl was so eager that he should be happy. She'd agreed to the improvements Edward thought essential: new plumbing, electrical overhauling, a brand-new kitchen and upstairs bathroom, the downstairs one modernized, order introduced to the garden, total abolishment of frilly muddle, the dining-room put to its proper use. Would the landlord agree to the structural things? Sibyl had laughed a joyous yes.

It was all still exactly the same, just six years tattier. The dining-room still Sibyl's junk room. Guests ate from their laps or from side tables or stood round the sideboard juggling with not enough hands. Edward had grown used to letting things slide.

He'd have a divan in here, cleanly Scandinavian. To toss around thoughts on. Mull over angles. He saw the room as it would be: a clean, bare, creative haven.

He'd left the work for Sibyl to put in hand because she knew good local tradesmen and was on the spot. Edward daydreamed in his rut: Elizabeth Bay to his tenth-floor office and back. Saw himself and Sibyl and two lovely children in the house sparkling inside and outside; the parents creative, the children studious, guests intelligent and appreciative. It was so real it was hard to wait for its reality. A week without her was endless.

He'd had to wait for her visits. She wouldn't let him go there till the work was done. She wouldn't let him make love to her until they started life together with everything ready. Think how much more *marvellous* it would be.

One thought had persisted behind his dreaming, and once when she came to town he said, 'From now on I'll take over the rent.'

Sibyl laughed. 'Darling sugar, there's no *rent.*'

'How d'you mean?'

'I mean it's *ours,* a gift from the parents, darling.'

He hadn't even met them. Sibyl called them the parents. Separately they were Mummy and Daddy. Edward could afford his own land, would have liked to choose it with Sibyl; he knew Strachan & Wykeham would underwrite building costs. He didn't like the feeling of obligation.

'I know why you've got that funny look and your eyes have gone all haggard.' She stroked his face. 'You couldn't be more *wrong,* sugar, there's no obligation at *all.*'

So Edward had felt it the more deeply.

Sibyl said leave it to her when he asked how the work was going. He liked her air of authority, felt relieved that she was there to watch over things. She wasn't tied down to a regular job as he was. She made quite a bit from her pots, she said. The brick pottery he'd looked at with its cold kiln and its clutter, the dusty heaps of broken clay and bits of wobbly glazed stuff, was because she'd been staying with Diana. Sometimes he felt like surprising her at the house, but he didn't dare.

Yet without her anxiety flourished. He rang her often. Each time he wanted to ask about the house, each time remained tongue-tied for fear of annoying her. Sibyl bubbled over with so many interests. In time he'd learned that those interests took precedence. That every day brought fresh absorbing problems, and items already on Sibyl's agenda had to wait. Then her pots she couldn't let slide. Edward understood all this now. He knew she'd meant to get work on the house started. He'd grown to know about Sibyl's crowded days.

One Saturday she drove in so Edward could take her to lunch, and afterwards came back to his flat. She allowed one kiss for his surge of passion then sat facing him with a cigarette.

'You'll never guess,' she said.

He'd thought it would be the renovations near completion.

'The parents keep asking when the wedding's to be.'

Edward smiled in collusion.

'Of course we could pretend we had but they'd think it sneaky, I mean, why behind their *backs,* they'd think, and then the strain on *us* when they popped in loaded with *questions.*'

'That's not likely, is it?' Edward said.

'Well, it's less than two hundred kilometres and they move around quite a bit and I'm all they've *got.*'

'You're all I've got too,' Edward said. He'd wanted her very much at that moment.

'It's just they pop *in,* sugar, they're mad about springing *surprises.*'

They sounded hell. 'Doesn't seem reason enough for doing something you're so dead against. We won't grow horns or warts being unmarried.'

Sibyl laughed, then grew serious. 'But what *difference* does it make? We don't have to let it *bug* us. All I mean is why upset them when it's so easy not to? And with Daddy's leg.'

Edward knew Daddy had a gammy leg – pain and a permanent limp – from an accident got in his former trucking business. He was silent. He felt a mite stifled. He couldn't see what Daddy's leg had to do with it. He wanted to marry her, had wanted to from the start. Yet there was the feeling of being first tricked out of it and now tricked into it.

Sibyl pounced into his hesitation. 'If it were just *us,* darling – no one deplores ghastly old marriage more than *I* do – but you know, well, I'd *hate* to hurt them.'

He understood that. Sibyl was close to her parents. He'd

like parents he was close to. Of course he wanted to marry her. What a smoker she was.

'Especially after the house,' Sibyl said, 'and being so happy I've found someone to share it with.'

'I've wanted us to marry all along,' Edward said.

'So've I, *deep down.*'

He'd thought her childish underlining of words one of the most endearing things about her.

He'd pictured them in the house while she lit a new cigarette. But it wasn't the house of his daydreams, it was the real house with its built-in look of someone's continuous living. 'How long've you had it?' he asked.

'The house? Gosh, darling, for *ever* practically.'

So the parents' gift wasn't for him. 'Whose name is it in?'

'Well, *mine,* darling.'

'Mind if we change it to joint ownership?'

Sibyl laughed. 'What's mine is yours and vee versa, I hope.'

'I'd rather,' Edward said.

'Well, all right – I can't see *why,* darling.'

Edward knew he sounded a stuffy prig when he said, 'I'm not a pauper.'

'Oh, *darling!*' She smiled at the child he was. 'Such a lot of *fuss.*'

She'd won of course, simply by putting it off.

Edward jumped when the door of the bare room opened. 'Aren't you ever coming to *bed,* darling?' It was cold cream night. No doubt because of tomorrow's luncheon guests.

CHAPTER IV

Lindsay was already twenty minutes late, but today Edward felt indulgent. It might be the furniture he'd selected during an overlong lunch hour, and the charcoal carpet. And a deadlock for the door so Sibyl couldn't burst into his concentration. Perhaps it was the weather; there'd been some bits of blue. But he knew it was the angles on Lindsay's thing that had sprouted all day long. Once started they grew on each other and he'd jotted each down as it came. Just having something on paper gave him confidence. Out on his furnishing spree, for instance, he hadn't let himself be intimidated, hadn't felt the usual derisive eyes picking holes in his purchases. Today he'd been easy and assured.

For a start he'd suggest detailed fieldwork to Lindsay. Would Lindsay come up with anything? Had Lindsay thought of dramatizing the film? There wouldn't be much Lindsay hadn't thought of, but the fact he'd roped Edward in at all meant he wanted all the help he could get. Two heads were better than one. Lindsay had yet to get the right people even interested, let alone land the financial backing. Maybe Lindsay always worked this way: sounded out non-writers whose cultural appreciation covered a wide spectrum. Edward the choice this time.

Lindsay was busy on a trilogy of television plays. He was about halfway through the second. Probably so engrossed he hadn't noticed the time. Edward couldn't think of a more rewarding life. The satisfaction Lindsay must feel, the sense of achievement. Edward tried hard not to feel the usual envy. He wouldn't speak sharply to Lindsay today as he had on Friday. Lindsay had a lot of talent or he wouldn't be so successful. Edward would show his gratitude by giving Lindsay all the co-operation he could.

He was pleased with the notes he'd made. They were ready on his desk and as Edward wandered about the office his eyes kept returning to them. After the down of yesterday – the whole week-end in fact – it was remarkable the way ideas had seemed to flow today. Lindsay said writing was bloody hard work, but Edward secretly believed in bursts of brilliance. Secretly, too, he'd like to be better than Lindsay, come up with a film of his own. Or a novel. Or something. A fantasy could come true.

He stood at the window. A thousand windows faced him from other office towers.

Yesterday's lunch had gone on nearly six hours. The Spensers and Cliffords arrived with mud and umbrellas around eleven-thirty. Nance brought a soggy quiche, but not the two boys who had something better to do, it seemed. Small mercies. The Spensers had the smartest house in the district, a lot of stained timber and a glass and inner court-yards, big swimming pool and arranged trees. Sibyl said it wasn't a patch on theirs. Max was in advertising display and Julie editorial assistant to a textbooks publisher. They had no children. They had a routine. They were on top of their lives.

Sibyl made her old standby: goulash with rice. She could always rely on Edward to see to people's drinks and ash-trays. Max, Julie and Nance were cigarettes, Jeff his pipe. All disgusting, but Sibyl was worst of all. She would balance a lighted cigarette on the edge of a table and often forget it was there. And often when she stubbed a cigarette it remained smouldering until Edward killed it off. She was such good company, easy to get along with, full of easy laughter; and that all took time. It was Edward in his quiet way who kept a semblance of order. People took his ministrations for granted; only Nance always thanked him with her friendly smile and a quick nervous glance from her grey eyes.

He didn't know why, but suddenly yesterday Sibyl's pots put his teeth on edge. It might have been all the enthusiastic talk about her exhibition, started by Jeff. Edward had always loved it that Sibyl was a potter. 'My wife's a ceramics artist.' He heard himself proudly saying that to people. Had he ever? During the goulash balanced on knees Jeff had got down to tintacks: he'd made a provisional gallery booking for June next year. That gave Sibyl seven clear months, and was Thursday okay to bring the gallery man to see samples of Sibyl's work? Jeff's word was good enough, but Jeff would rather the proprietor saw for himself. And Jeff intended to keep Sibyl's nose to the grindstone.

Sibyl looked at Edward. 'What do *you* think, darling, think I'll make it?'

Edward shrugged and smiled and said, 'Whatever you think,' and thought how she always asked for his opinion or agreement, but would do as she wanted anyway. Quick, rushing, wilful, forgetful, and always so generously sorry afterwards. Coming back into the living-room after stacking the dishes and getting the percolator going, Edward had sat unnoticed by the window and watched Sibyl's animation. How she loved people. They were all smoking again with their clean ashtrays.

Sibyl didn't bother with her appearance; it had got her through so far, she said, so it could manage the rest. Animation was her saving grace, with the thick shiny chestnut hair in a bob. She was thin but graceful, with very good slim legs. Freckles, light blue eyes, a weathering skin. Small pointy nose, wide mouth, deep laughter lines at mouth and eyes. Thin neck beginning to look scraggy. Was it because her voice was high and light that she found it necessary to emphasize?

They'd left Sibyl's show undecided and were back on their old hobby horse, berating the government (State or National?) for doing something or leaving it undone. The cats had a lap each. Their talk stifled him, their endless circling round the unending problems. It was just then Sibyl's pots had got on his nerves: the messy ashtrays mocked their zeal, while the hopeless reforms it was all about kept Sibyl's kiln cold for weeks at a stretch.

Edward took their coffee in and drank his own in the kitchen. Wine was still flowing and its smell with the smoke had given him a headache. He put the things in the dishwasher to do later. All we need now, he'd thought, is the parents to pop in. He'd taken the vacuum cleaner upstairs to do the bedroom. Their voices had followed, loud with drink and argument. So he'd gone into his room and shut the door. Already it was 'his' room. High ceiling, a good size, almost as big as their bedroom. It was to have been the guest room but they never got round to that. It became very hot summer afternoons with the western sun. With the door shut their voices were far away. Engrossed in work he wouldn't hear them at all. He left the door open because the room smelled a bit musty. The windows had to be kept shut for the rain.

He took the vacuum cleaner into the bedroom, then saw he'd have to dust first. The house was always dusty, sometimes really dirty. About once every two months Sibyl got stuck into it, but it was Edward who did the stairs and hall regularly, and the kitchen and upstairs bathroom. Sibyl laughed at him: 'Goodness, sugar, what's a speck of dust in the total pollution?' But Sibyl knew it was bad enough for people to notice, especially Julie Spenser. Hence the frills and doodahs, the rugs and cushions, that were all meant to conceal. The pictures had been almost stuck to the walls with a pasty grime, but now Edward dusted them once a week. Edward spent a lot of time on housework. But from now on, he thought, as he cleaned up Sibyl's mess on the dressing-table, he'd need that time for Lindsay's thing. Just keep his own room clean.

They'd hung around till fiveish. Edward had felt worn

out. Not with the work he'd done but with waiting for them
to go. The ashtrays were spilling over because he hadn't
been there to replace them. He'd stood with Sibyl under
the back portico smiling goodbye.

Then going inside she said they'd heard him at housework.

'Just a bit,' Edward said.

'Well, just because you're such a dreamboat I'm going
to do you the most *scrumptious* new recipe I've been hoard-
ing with that beef you got yesterday.'

Lindsay was over an hour late. Edward sat down and
looked at his notes. Then again at his watch.

It was unfair to resent Sibyl. He knew that. He loved
her. She loved him, he knew that too. He'd be lost without
her. He liked her to have a life of her own. She was careless and thoughtless but she meant well. The poor girl
had done nothing potwise all week-end.

Ecology is the science of the relationships between organisms and their environments. Also called bionomics. Did
Lindsay know this? Probably, he had only to look in a
dictionary.

Up in his room with the table and chair waiting for the
scrumptious recipe he'd stared at his bare notepad, then
through the window at the housing development. He'd done
nothing for the meeting with Lindsay. He'd have long
curtains to the floor, something to let in the light but
screen the dispiriting view. And keep the summer sun
out.

Had she called him sugar before they were married? Or
had he been too in love to care?

'Christ, old boy, sorry.'

Edward jumped.

'Didn't see the bloody clock.' Lindsay was sober.

'It's all right.' Edward smiled. 'I know how busy you
are. I haven't been idle.' He saw Lindsay's eyes flicker
over his notes and added casually, 'A few ideas I jotted

down over the week-end.'

Lindsay didn't look scruffy today. He looked thoughtful and competent. He didn't have his briefcase. He sat
facing Edward. 'Sibyl come good?'

'Some,' Edward said. He could never tell Lindsay Sibyl's
opinion of him, and Lindsay was too conceited to see for
himself.

'Like what?'

Edward looked at his notes. He wanted to go along
with Lindsay and win his approbation, while at the same
time keep something for himself. He already had that
sorted out. He spoke quickly with a new note of authority,
keeping his eyes on his notes.

'I think leave the sea alone. Keep it simple. Start with
a plant, just one plant in relation to its environment. Then
how the process applies to all plants. Briefly explain the
pecking order. Point out how plants and animals are
so interdependent that investigation of one involves the
other. Deal with autecology and synecology, bring in
climate, soil, temperature, humidity, quality of light, sort
of food and so on. Some lab shots of scientific study, then
the whole combined effect in forests, deserts, rivers, lakes,
swamps and so on. Leave the sea, just make it clear the
same applies. The sea's still largely a mystery, in any
case.'

Edward stopped and looked at Lindsay. Lindsay was
hunched and staring at the floor, smoking in quick puffs.
He said without moving, 'This Sibyl's stuff?'

'We talked about it together.'

Lindsay looked at Edward. His lips were pursed. 'It's
pretty general. Any ideas about shaping it?'

'Shaping it?'

'Like you said, the form. That's where the bloody work
comes in – look, what about a bite to eat?'

Edward was thrilled at the invitation. It meant Lindsay
wasn't bored, wasn't scornful of Edward's ideas. He found

them worth exploring. The cleaners were about, in any case; one had already poked a frown into Edward's office.

They walked to a bloody good steakhouse Lindsay knew with a bar so you could get a drink first. It was great to be going to dinner with Lindsay. Edward thought how great it would be if someone important Lindsay knew saw them together, conferring, tossing around ideas. The shape, he thought, the form! He must come up with something. Lindsay wouldn't expect it tonight, at least Edward hoped not. Then he thought he'd get on to the electrician tomorrow, perhaps call in there on his way to town; with any luck the man could come tomorrow night and plan Edward's requirements for his room. Lindsay was talking about his play; he'd got bloody stuck at a crucial point and that's when he'd seen the bloody time.

Lindsay had whisky, Edward gin and tonic. It was a poky place done in dark red walls and upholstery and black-stained timber. The red made Edward think of blood, but it might be its being a steakhouse plus Lindsay's stream of bloodys. The lights were red and dim, very Sibyl-ish, perhaps with the same purpose.

They got a miniscule corner for two. Lindsay's weedy body looked at ease but Edward was hampered by his muscly build. Lindsay did the ordering, including a bottle of the most expensive claret. Then he grinned at Edward. 'Bloody famished,' he said, and lit a cigarette. He looked around and waved to a group of men through the dimness, the din and smoke.

Edward plunged. 'Have you thought of dramatizing it?'

'Christ, yes, hold the thing together, otherwise you get a dull bloody science thing, no popular appeal. Good thinking on your part, old boy.'

'Thanks,' Edward said casually, the excitement inside.

'Fictional family,' Lindsay said. 'Human interest. Means you can have the ecology bit on the side and still get the suckers.'

The waiter came with the wine and its ritual. Then the food. Lindsay fell on it ravenously, then with bulging mouth snatched the French mustard and plonked a great daub on his wooden platter.

Edward picked up knife and fork. 'I think perhaps it sounds back to front, or upside down perhaps. I think ecology should take precedence. I don't mean not keep the human interest but turn it the other way round.'

Lindsay was buttering his roll, sending flakes of crust all over the place, one into Edward's lap. 'Might be something in that.' But his dubious voice saw nothing in it. 'Toss it around and see what you come up with.'

'All right, thanks.' Edward's smile for Lindsay was warm. There was a longish silence. 'You haven't worked it out yet, then?' Edward said.

Lindsay said in a loud bullying voice, making heads turn, 'Look, old boy, I'm doing a bloody trilogy – I'm relying on you a lot on this little caper.'

'I didn't mean – '

'Just use your bloody head.'

Edward was silent. He hated arguments. He mustn't criticize Lindsay. Lindsay was the expert. He hated the way Lindsay gobbled food and swallowed good wine as though it were water. Edward was still at the start of his steak and Lindsay was just about finished.

Edward said, 'I like your fictional family.'

'Fine, old boy.' Lindsay lolled back with a toothpick and looked about him in a bored way.

Edward felt a surge of panic. He mustn't bore Lindsay, mustn't lose out on this miracle. He should have kept talking, throwing ideas around. He made his voice terribly casual. 'Know what I was wondering?'

'Shoot.'

'Whether you can lend me an old script so I can see how it's put down.' A phrase of Lindsay's came into his head. 'Get the visual hang,' he added.

'Sure, old boy, if you think it'll help. I'll bring a couple along.' He looked at his watch. 'Christ, that the bloody time? Got a date with Diana.' He turned and began snapping his fingers for the bill, saying to Edward over his shoulder, 'Don't mind, old boy, do you? No need for you to leave, finish your grub and coffee.'

Edward was shattered. The steak in his mouth tasted like sawdust. 'That's quite all right,' he said.

The waiter brought the bill and Lindsay put two ten-dollar notes on the dish. 'Entertainment expenses,' he said with a wink at Edward, 'your department, old boy.'

Edward smiled. Lindsay wiped his entire face with the blood-red napkin. 'Well, we've a long way to go,' he said. 'Tell you what – make this today's little project, work out the family element. Like a go at it?'

'Very much,' Edward said. He tried to keep his disappointment from showing.

They arranged to meet in Edward's office the following Friday. Lindsay got up with a casual, 'See you then, then,' and started threading his way out.

The next moment he was back. 'Look, old boy, I'm a bit low, can you manage a twenty till Friday?'

So that was it. The bite to eat an elaborate build-up to a bite of a different kind. 'Of course.' Edward got the bill out and Lindsay snatched it.

'Friday then.' He moved away and yelled back, '*Avec* script.'

Edward ordered coffee. He couldn't swallow more food. He was ashamed of his suspicion. Lindsay would have asked straight out in the office for a loan. He'd borrowed money before. Sometimes he remembered to repay it, sometimes Edward had to remind him. Lindsay was casual about money and Edward thought that unless he said something he might not get the twenty back. That didn't worry him. What did worry him was Lindsay's reaction to his ideas. A bored look appeared on Lindsay's face at anything Edward said. Lindsay knew Edward's experience was nil, yet he'd asked for Edward's help and still seemed to want it. Shouldn't Lindsay be more encouraging, more ready to analyse Edward's suggestions so Edward could understand what made them good or bad? Or made them bad? Judging by Lindsay's response Edward's attempts so far were laughable. He felt both resentful and disappointed and it was hard to know which feeling was the stronger. Perhaps distrust of Lindsay was stronger than both.

Edward suspected Lindsay would secretly note his ideas. Not *pinch* them, as Sibyl said, but just take note of them. Lindsay had an excellent memory. Edward knew Lindsay pretty well. When Lindsay made a dubious face it meant he saw something in an idea that he could use. Lindsay didn't miss a trick. He discarded nothing until he'd wrung it dry.

Diana. That had gone on a long time. As long as him and Sibyl. The difference being Lindsay had his own creative place and no parents popping in on whims.

Edward paid for his coffee and walked to his car park. The rain was still holding off but the air felt heavy with it. Traffic was thinned out. He'd come up with quite a bit today, he thought, but he'd kept a lot in reserve. Just as well, the way things had turned out. For instance, how could you fit ecology into an hour? Wasn't the theme too big unless you did it Edward's way, starting with one example? It was a subject that led itself on from one thing to another, on and on. Where did you stop? Uranium, for instance. Uranium was a metallic element found in several minerals, and therefore, where it occurred, part of the ecology. But it was also a most profitable commodity so where did that lead you? To nuclear power and undisposable deadly waste; to mass-destructive bombs and nations perilously juggling and to Sibyl's leave-it-in-the-earth campaign. You could introduce your audience to ecology as a subject, and even though a proportion of them might be way ahead of you there was something of value in putting the idea into visual form. You'd help in spreading the alert. Did Lindsay have the slightest inkling? Yet even if you got the urgency across, was there any point anyway when power in the world was in the small tight grip of self-interest?

All going our own blind way to destruction, Edward thought. Then thought, hell-bent. Then thought, at least Lindsay's thing is making me think, making me see what Sibyl's on about.

Surprise, surprise: Sibyl was home. She'd done roast lamb, using Edward's mint for the sauce.

Edward kissed her hair. 'Sorry, darling, Lindsay suggested eating while we nutted it out.'

Sibyl wasn't a bit put out. She cleared Edward's place from the table. 'Did you say Lindsay's doing this on *spec*?'

'Yes.'

'Doesn't sound *at all* like Lindsay.'

'Why not, with his reputation? He can afford to take a punt.'

Edward felt suddenly immensely amiable. He was brimful of ideas, and there was Lindsay's continuing interest: in his offhand way Lindsay *had* been encouraging. And there was the furniture for his room. And Lindsay's borrowing. Edward wouldn't mind at all if Lindsay forgot to repay it, and wished the loan had been bigger.

CHAPTER V

Soon after Edward got home on Tuesday the electrician came. 'Nice weather for ducks,' he said, smiling.

For once Edward was glad Sibyl was out; she'd have wanted a say in his wiring. She'd told him for once, some urgency about world famine.

Upstairs Edward explained what he wanted. He and the electrician worked things out together and Edward enjoyed it. The man, whose name was Forshaw, estimated he could get the job done within a week. 'Let's say today week she'll be finished.' His quote seemed reasonable to Edward for the times, and considering it included all the fitments.

He suggested a drink. Down in the kitchen Forshaw had beer, Edward gin and tonic.

'How's Mrs Piper?' Forshaw asked with a smile Edward found offensive.

'She's fine.'

'Still putting the world to rights?' The electrician knew Sibyl well (who didn't?) but this was his first meeting with Edward.

Edward didn't want to have to endure this sort of talk about Sibyl, so he said, 'Know a good locksmith around? I've a deadlock I want on the door.'

'Simple,' Forshaw said, 'I'll do the job in a twinkling.'

Edward got the deadlock and Forshaw said, 'Back door or front?'

'The room you've been measuring,' Edward said and felt his face go warm. 'It's a study, you see, privacy, sometimes children are here.' He resented his need to explain.

'Okeydoke.' They returned upstairs. Edward got his tools but Forshaw had some. It took more than a twinkling but it was a good thing to have done. Edward studied the printed instructions and diagrams while Forshaw got the lock on.

He went downstairs with Forshaw and saw him off. He must remember to ask Sibyl to be home when Forshaw came in the morning. He got a fresh gin and tonic and went back up to his room, jingling the deadlock's keys in his pocket. Before going into his room he got his keyring from the bedroom and put the new keys on it. He'd carry it with him always from now on.

He liked the crosses Forshaw had put on the walls and skirting with his thick pencil. He thought of the furniture and tried to estimate where each piece would go. There wasn't much. He should have measured the room before buying the furniture although he'd had a rough idea from the measurements he'd made for the carpeting. He wouldn't have to worry about glare once the curtains were up and the indirect lighting. A stenographer at Strachan & Wykeham's had told him once, he couldn't think why, that it was best to have the light coming from the left. So his desk would go here, facing the wall, with the windows to his left. He'd have a calendar on the wall, maybe a small, choice, ecological sort of painting he'd buy from a gallery. The divan on the other side. The divan was locally made but done in Scandinavian style, nothing more than an elegant platform with a foam all-over cushion covered in sombre green. He'd have a pile of cushions. He'd better start jotting things down as he thought of them. His blank notepad was still on the table with the pencil and Edward wrote 'cushions' on it. Then he added in brackets, 'muted greens and browns'.

The filing cabinet could go next to the desk. It wasn't really a filing cabinet, just a piece of furniture from the same expensive place where he'd got the divan and book-shelves. Roughly one and a half metres high, sixty cm wide, with a mixture of drawers and open recesses. Or maybe the bookshelves there and the filing thing in the corner of the window wall. The deep, comfortable, costly leather armchair could go anywhere, it was on nylon runners and could be pushed with a finger.

Excitement rose in his throat. As soon as Forshaw had finished next Tuesday the carpet could be laid. He'd phone them tomorrow and make a firm date and ask Sibyl to be home; he'd write it down for her just to make sure.

He sat on the dining chair at the table and sketched an

arrangement of furniture. Then another. He was still there trying variations when he heard Sibyl's voice coming upstairs.

'You home, Eddie?'

'In here.'

She pushed the door. 'For heaven's *sake*!' Then she saw the new lock. 'What's this?'

'Just a lock.'

'I can see that, I mean *why*?'

He stood up, smiling. 'Just for when I'm working, darling, for when your women bring kiddies.'

'I see — *gosh*, they *don't*. You had dinner?'

'Yes.' He hadn't, he'd forgotten all about it, his room had been sustenance enough. 'See these crosses?'

'Yes?'

'The electrician. He's coming in the morning. Around ten. Can you be here to let him in?'

'Oh, gosh, not *tomorrow,* darling. Tomorrow of *all* days. Big joint meeting in the Town Hall bang on ten o'clock.'

'D'you have to be there?'

'Of *course* I do.'

'Can't it go on without you for once?'

'Dear God, Eddie, it's *world famine* — don't you *care*?'

Edward turned away from her stricken light blue eyes. Of course he cared, he just wasn't going to care at her behest, and never if she called him Eddie.

'I thought you had to get down to your potting,' he said.

'Of *course* I have, I *must,* I had tomorrow all mapped out for a big firing day.' Then suddenly her voice was soft and close. 'Don't sulk, sugar.' Her arms went round him.

'I'm not sulking.' He held her tight. 'I just think you've got to remember now that I'm doing something too, with far less time to do it in.'

'I *know,* darling, I *am,* I *do*, it's just that it's something so terribly *important* and *brinkish*.'

'So is ecology,' Edward said.

'How about if I leave the door open for him with a note?' Sibyl said.

'We'll think of something.'

They watched an old movie on television. Sibyl fell asleep while it was on. They didn't often watch television. But from now on Edward wanted to catch the news every day. For anything ecologically brinkish.

Wednesday morning Edward phoned the office and told Miss Goldman he'd be a bit late because of the dentist. Sibyl went off to her big joint meeting and Edward let in Mr Forshaw who came a bit before ten with a young assistant. Both men wore white overalls. Forshaw promised to shut the study when they left. Edward didn't want Sibyl pulling his wires about, but mostly he wanted the transformation complete before she saw the room. Edward gave Forshaw one of his precious keys so he could get in tomorrow.

In the office he phoned the carpet people; their men could come at nine in the morning on Friday week. That would give him time to clean up after Forshaw finished on Tuesday. He realized he'd have to take the carpet Friday off so he'd be there to keep Sibyl at bay. Mr Strachan wouldn't mind. Sibyl could get busy in the pottery and maybe get the shopping done for once.

At lunch time he went to the curtains department of a big store and chose one from their most expensive range of fabrics. It was just right, Edward felt: almost white yet greyish, substantial enough to hang well but with a weave he could see through. The woman tried to bully him into having them lined, but Edward knew what he wanted: a screen against the sun that would let in the light, plus a sense of privacy. He chose a thick white rod with acorns and big rings. One of their experts would come to take measurements on the carpet-laying day, and when the curtains were made they'd come again and install them.

On his way through the store a display of typewriters caught his eye. Then and there he bought an Olympia portable and a ream of foolscap paper (Lindsay used foolscap), and loved the weighty feel of them as he pushed through crowds back to his office. Again and again through the afternoon his eyes went to the typewriter looking so professional in its case down by the wall behind his chair. The furniture could come the week after next when the carpet was down and the electrical work completed. He'd have to be there for that too. No doubt Sibyl would laugh at his secretive preparations, make a guessing game of them, but for Edward the room's completion was the essential starting-point. He could never muddle through the way Sibyl did. He'd proved that at the week-end.

Just as importantly, these unilateral decisions gave him a sense of identity he'd never had. Even meeting Lindsay and marrying Sibyl hadn't filled the real lack in his life. This was the sort of personal stimulation he craved. And best of all, the week's crowning excitement, was another session with Lindsay coming up Friday, because Lindsay's thing was the peg everything hung upon.

When he got home Edward went straight upstairs with the typewriter and paper. It was great having his own door to unlock. He put the precious things on the little table. Sibyl was home, she'd yelled hello from the kitchen. He saw with satisfaction the progress Forshaw had made.

Sibyl was full of her meeting, she talked all through the grilled chops, broccoli and carrots, then through the Danish Blue. They'd had a wonderful response, and lots of promises of community action. Sibyl never asked what Edward had been doing because he never did anything; in any case she was full of her own affairs. While she got the coffee ready Edward cleared away, rinsed and stacked the dishes.

Sibyl laughed. 'Gosh, aren't we *efficient*!'

'Working tonight, darling.' He gave her a hug in passing.

He took his coffee upstairs. The door locked itself neatly
behind him. He played about with the typewriter, getting
the feel of it. He'd typed an envelope now and again in
the office, alone there. At the top of a sheet of foolscap he
typed *Here is my Space,* then underneath, *by Lindsay
Reid.* Then lower down, *Here is my Space,* and below it,
by Edward Piper. Then he remembered *Heritage and
Outrage,* and typed that in capitals, and followed it with
by Edward Piper, also in capitals. He liked the look of
the last one, it had more authority. It looked worthier,
weightier : Edward Piper as a name looked more solid
than Lindsay Reid. Lindsay Reid was a thin, flimsy name.
He remembered he'd had a thought on the way home; he'd
been held up at some red lights just as the rain started again,
and he'd thought by that to remember and now he couldn't
think what the rain starting had been to remind him of.
Or had it been the hold-up, the red lights? Once the room
was done thought would be organized too. Imagine Lindsay
writing under these conditions – that was a laugh.

He put the cover on the typewriter and sat with some
sheets of foolscap in front of him. He didn't much like
Lindsay's fictional family. What did Lindsay mean –
Mum, Dad and the kids, laughter and tears, sunshine and
shadow? A young married couple perhaps, Edward
thought, newlyweds say, wanting a new world, or rather
a conserved, protected world – and what could be newer
than that? Lindsay wouldn't like a young married couple,
they didn't sound like Lindsay. Lindsay laughed at upwards-and-outwards, eyes on the future and so on. Funny
Lindsay should choose ecology at all.

When Sibyl knocked around ten-thirty Edward got up
at once. Sibyl tried to peer past him but Edward slipped
out quickly and shut the door.

'Affairs of state?' She laughed. 'Thought you might like a drink or something.'

'Only something,' Edward said, embracing her and smiling over her shoulder at his deadlock.

They made love that night. Edward felt on a peak and flowing with magnanimity. Creative people must always feel like this. Afterwards Sibyl fell asleep at once, as she always did. He looked at her dear familiar profile. He saw himself the man, Sibyl the woman, superior people, creative. Their beautiful son following in Edward's footsteps. A noble trio concerned for their world and its people, the ecological theme carrying the son into danger, floods perhaps, and father rescuing him in the nick of time while the rain beat down in ever fiercer ferocity. Fiercer ferocity. Fiercer ferocity? Edward slipped from Sibyl's bed and went to his own, clinging to drowsiness and the dream-theme.

But he was wide awake. His thoughts grew bitter about the son he'd never have. It had been another of Sibyl's shocks: no children. He'd learned about her first brief rotten marriage (shock enough) on their wedding day, but he hadn't known about her defective reasoning, the steely quality of it. It had come up casually over Nance's two boys, when Sibyl in careless cruelty had said he'd never know the joys of fatherhood unless he chose a surrogate mother. Not wanting children, at once he'd felt deprived. Why should the decision be Sibyl's? He hated to remember the scene.

Sibyl joking. 'Think of the *saving*, sugar.' But she'd seen his resentment and had gone on soberly, 'It's evil to add another munching mouth. Just think of the millions starving and you'll find it's not important, just male vanity.'

Edward had said, 'You've been dishonest about a number of things.'

And Sibyl bridling. 'Dis*honest*? *Me*?' Then in her generous way saying, 'I admit I should have discussed it with you but I thought you knew my views – and anyway, darling, you've never *displayed* a rampant paternal instinct, *have* you?'

Edward's resentment had lasted a couple of days. A man had a right to a son. What was marriage for, just to mollify the parents? But resentment collapsed, and with it the want and the need and the right, and in their place the perfect boy and youth became a special and permanent factor in his daydreams, replacing the two lovely children of pre-marriage imaginings. Mostly he even forgot Sibyl's thoughtlessness, or trickery. It mattered now only because he was wide awake.

Morning brought a savage headache. Sibyl was used to Edward's silences and prattled her way through breakfast. He took two aspirin and left for the office. He hoped Forshaw would respect the privacy of his room. Short of saying outright he didn't want Sibyl to see it Edward thought he'd made it plain enough to Forshaw. By lunch time his headache was gone and during the afternoon he was able to think creatively again.

Sibyl's gallery man came that day, with Jeff Clifford. The man *adored* her stuff, she said. Edward hadn't been in her pottery for months and thought she must have really done some work since his last depressing visit. She was excited and had stuffed and roasted a real chicken Jeff had brought from people on a farm who grew real ones.

'Forward together,' Edward said with a smile.

'You mean you're actually *getting* somewhere with Lindsay?'

Edward compressed his lips.

'Darling, I didn't mean – I only meant – '

'You never do mean, do you?'

'I only meant – well – *Lindsay*.'

'Forget it,' Edward said.

He ate without tasting. Sibyl for once was subdued. As

soon as he'd finished he went upstairs without lifting a finger to help. Forshaw had shut the door and Edward used his key.

He knew Sibyl didn't mean it. She didn't trust Lindsay, that's all it was. It was up to Edward to prove himself, prove Lindsay, prove them as a team. Then Sibyl would see.

Forshaw had made progress. Edward moved the chair to the window and sat looking at the housing development through the rain. Daylight saving seemed silly in this weather.

But next day his spirits rose at the imminent meeting with Lindsay. Proving Sibyl wrong about Lindsay had become part of the project; her bias was unfair and stupid, and especially disparaging of Edward's role. He didn't believe Sibyl meant to belittle him, it was just her unfeelingness. But all in all it added a sense of urgency. His head was agog with ideas; nothing on paper, just all inside ready to pour out. Even staid old Strachan gave him a second look when Edward had to confer over something. An approving look.

During the afternoon Lindsay rang. 'About today, old boy, afraid I can't make it.'

Edward's disappointment was so intense he couldn't speak.

'You there?' Lindsay said.

'Yes,' Edward said, then added, 'that's all right.'

'Sorry, old boy, something I can't get out of.'

'I said all right,' Edward said, trying not to grind it out.

'Monday, same time, your offices?'

'All right.'

He went home depressed. He told Sibyl he was going to work all week-end, come what may. Sibyl made no reply. Dinner was a silent meal.

He knew he should feel excited about the electrical wires

looped round the room in and out of the electrician's holes. He sat at the little table and listened to the rain. It had held off all day, starting again just in time to drench the home-going workers. He'd bet Lindsay hadn't thought of the funny weather in ecological terms. Did Lindsay do any thinking at all when he was so caught up with girls and parties and drinking? He hadn't mentioned the loan.

The rain was making things grow that had never been known to grow before. The grass in their garden was just about waist-high. Edward had seen a newspaper item: Century's Strangest Weather. In it, even the cautious weather bureau conceded the weather was the most extraordinary of the century. Warmer oceans, rain-soaked arid areas, unusually frequent thunderstorms. People took things for granted. That was a point the film should make, the taking for granted of air and water and land. They'd been pulled up short over energy fuel, now they took even its shortage for granted. Lindsay took him for granted. If it had been Edward unable to keep the appointment he'd have been apologetic, concerned, eager to hear Lindsay's proguess. Lindsay had been none of those things. Lindsay took him too much for granted.

And didn't Sibyl? Sibyl took it for granted he'd go to the office every day year after year until age discarded him. Edward was just as concerned as Sibyl at nuclear proliferation but because Sibyl made all the noise about it she took it for granted that her concern was greater.

Edward felt very tired. He hadn't slept well lately. He went to bed around ten. Sibyl was still downstairs, or maybe out.

CHAPTER VI

The rain had stopped by morning. It was Saturday. Edward felt fine after nine hours' sleep. Out in the garden he smiled at the reasonable cats. The parsley was yellower and the rosemary dead but the mint was almost a jungle. He'd get a new rosemary. The parsley he'd nurse back to health.

He didn't mind the shopping Sibyl had forgotten because he could map out the work he'd do. In a week's time he'd be electrified and carpeted. With that thought buoying him he knew it would be a productive week-end and on Monday Lindsay would have to acknowledge his ability.

When he got back with the shopping the parents were there. They'd made an early start from their place near the Shoalhaven River so they'd have a longer day with Sibyl and Edward. Edward couldn't speak, submitting his cheek to Mummy's kiss with a twitch of a smile. The kitchen was full of them and their bags and parcels, including a V-neck steel-grey sleeveless pullover for Edward and a sickly pink sweater for Sibyl, both knitted by Mummy. Edward always felt stifled in their presence : Mummy twittering about idiotic local events with her pointy pink nose and woollies in all weathers, Daddy in his V-neck sleeveless pullovers winter and summer in every shade of grey, limping and hearty. Now the stifling was worse with his creative work so pressing.

There was no escape before lunch. He was pinioned by their cosy embracing talk. Lunch was a great mound of prawns they'd brought and Daddy's bottled beer. Edward disliked both but made a pretence of enjoying them. He noticed that Sibyl had Mummy's nose, luckily modified. There was a lot of talk about the weather and the possibility of the Shoalhaven flooding if the rain kept on. They were booked in for the night at a motel and tomorrow were pushing on up north. They travelled around a lot, life one long woolly holiday.

Edward insisted on clearing lunch, hoping they'd go to the living-room or to Sibyl's pottery to admire her creations. But they just sat on round the table, excited about Sibyl's exhibition and hoping she wasn't overstraining herself with all her noble works.

'Proud of her, son?' Daddy asked.

Edward nodded from the dishwasher he was stacking.

'Leave that, dear, I'll do it,' Mummy said.

'No. Really.' Edward didn't like Mummy's hands.

They didn't ask what exciting things Edward was doing. He switched the dishwasher on. At first, incredibly, they shouted over it, but about halfway through Sibyl said, 'Let's go somewhere quieter.' She threw a little smile at Edward and he saw that for once Sibyl was being considerate. When the dishwasher entered its last long silence Edward was still standing beside it, his mind an angry blank. At last it was done and he propped it ajar. He continued to stand there.

The stench of prawns hung about. One of the cats came in with a wistful mewing, scenting more of Mummy's earlier largesse. Edward sent it scooting out through the cat door, then returned and washed his hands at the sink. He had an idea and opened the refrigerator; clearly it hadn't been cleaned out since the last time he'd done it. He couldn't bear the sight of it and how else should he pass the time? He couldn't think, ideas were dead, he could never think when the parents were about. Joining them in the living-room was out of the question. He began removing the fridge's contents.

When he was at the washing stage Mummy came into the kitchen to make a pot of tea.

'Oh, my goodness, you dear boy, Sibyl *has* got a treasure.'

Edward smiled politely and kept on working. Mummy's eyes watched every movement until the kettle boiled. Then getting the tray ready she said, 'Coming in for a cuppa with us? – you don't want to upset Tom.' It was said with a smile but Edward detected reproach, maybe even a threat.

'Thanks very much but I can't leave this halfway and I really don't like tea after prawns.'

'Suit yourself, dear.' She went with the tray.

It was a long job and Edward spun it out longer. He'd just about done when they all trooped back to the kitchen, Sibyl and Mummy to start preparations for dinner, Daddy to stand in everyone's way pronouncing his limp and smile.

'Grass is long, son.'

'The rain,' Edward said. 'Like a drink?'

'Don't mind if I do.'

They went to the living-room. After all, he had only to listen. The tea tray was still there. Daddy talked about dairy farming and the government. He didn't have to keep Daddy going, Daddy kept going anyway. Somehow the time went. Sibyl came in and had a drink and sat on the arm of Daddy's armchair twiddling with his hair that was like Sibyl's but lighter, more of a red than chestnut. Sibyl looked pleased with herself. Mummy had taken over the kitchen.

Edward felt his eyes were glazed and also the brain behind them.

Dinner was awful. Mummy had overcooked the beef Edward had chosen with such care at the butcher's. There was no choice, just plates brimming with watery mashed pumpkin, unbrowned baked potatoes, pea pellets and a shroud of gravy over the lot. Edward hated gravy. He caught a commiserating look from Sibyl followed at once by a silencing frown. Did she expect an outburst? From good old Edward?

They went soon after coffee (Mummy had tea) because

as Daddy said it had been a long day and they had quite
a trip tomorrow. Edward stood with Sibyl in the road and
smiled them off into the clouds. Daddy told Edward he'd
better watch the mint or it'd take over. Edward left Sibyl
still waving and went back inside and straight up to his
room. His key, his room, his space. Here is my space.
Edward felt the sourness of his smile.

He sat at the table. He knew it was useless but at least
he was alone, there was peace. Then he felt panicky
because he had to come up with something for Lindsay on
Monday. Tomorrow for sure. Today was the parents' fault.
Tom and Rosemary Finch. In their fifties, small-minded,
self-centred. Tom was chunky and tough with big hands and
a rough and ready way of talking. Sibyl's light blue eyes,
freckles and laughter. And her incessant smoking. Self-
made, always right. Never grew tired of recounting the
good deal he'd made in selling his trucking business, or
the investments in land that followed. Always free with
advice, knew with a laugh what was best for everybody.
Rosemary a faded brownish woman, hair, eyes, skin all
brown, just the pink nose that grew red with excitement.
Not a thought in her head, echoed Tom's views; no stimulation in either of them.

Edward had a tall, leafy, slender plant growing from the
bottom to the top of a sheet of foolscap. He began to add
more leaves. He heard the distant crash of crockery.

They doted on Sibyl, especially Tom, who saw as daugh-
terly virtues his own defects of character. But despite all
that had happened – the awful wedding day, the letdowns
through the years – Edward knew Sibyl as basically loving
and generous. Even on their wedding day.

He'd felt like a supernumerary. The parents, their friends,
their little church, Sibyl's friends. Sibyl had said, 'What
about *your* friends, darling?' 'There's no one really,' he'd
said, because Lindsay who was going to be best man got
all tied up at the last minute and Edward had a stranger.

Everything taken care of : the wedding ring (Sibyl's grand-mother's), his future role, where he'd live. But his loneli-ness too, and he loved her for that. Everything about her he loved: her laughter and pots, her freckles and cats, her legs and hair and crazy emphases. Even the parents on the big day, although they were fond of him only as Sibyl's choice.

The wedding was for her parents, in their little church. Edward felt he'd been had and knew the feeling was un-worthy. He'd never been happy and this was happiness, he told himself. Sibyl had submitted to their hidebound ideas because they loved her so and she couldn't hurt them. It was a widespread but close community and the wedding a social event. Ceremony, speeches, breakfast had all been a trial for Edward. Sibyl's friends ribbing her : 'You'll never pot for posterity now'; 'What price citizens' rights bent all day over a hot stove?'; 'Who landed who, Sib?' Edward hated their humour, and didn't like to think of the aspects of Sibyl it revealed. He didn't like Sibyl's mother saying how thankful she was that Sibyl didn't have to uproot her life in Fernydale. And her father's puzzling remark with a patronizing smile and a clap on the shoulder: 'Well, she can't pick *two* bad eggs.'

Almost it was the parents' honeymoon because Tasmania was their suggestion.

In the plane Edward had asked what her father meant about two bad eggs. Sibyl had laughed. 'Oh, he must have meant Terry.' Then seeing his questioning face, 'I was married before, darling, I try to forget it, an absolute *pig,* I divorced him before a year was up, I'm sorry Daddy said anything.' Then to his silence she'd said, 'I'm sorry, darling.' Then, in an even softer voice, pressing against him, 'I'm sorry it's all been so *awful* for you today.'

The foolscap page was filled with leaves. Edward went on squeezing in more; tiny ones.

The house had been a wedding gift to Sibyl and Terry.

Edward just a latecomer. Even on their honeymoon Edward wondered what Sibyl saw in him, what gain was in it for her, and prayed he wouldn't turn out an absolute *pig,* or more likely absolute *millstone.* He knew now. Sibyl said it was love, she loved him, and that was true. But another truth was she liked to be married. All her friends were married, the parents liked her married, she liked a certified host when she was hostess, she liked his usefulness around the house, she liked to parade him, mention him among other absorbing occupations she had.

Sibyl knocked on his door, then tried the handle. 'Darling, why *locked*?'

Edward held his breath.

'*Do* open up, sugar, something terribly exciting.'

Edward drew another leaf. What was a lock for? Sibyl must understand that when his door was shut it meant he was working and not to be disturbed.

A fusillade of knocks. Then, 'Oh Eddie, I'm *bursting* with it.'

That was all. Here endeth the first lesson, Edward thought. He wished the divan were here so he could stretch out, maybe even stay all night on it. Instead, he put his head on his arms on the little table.

On Sunday Edward woke late. He'd crawled to bed around two after a series of naps at the table, each increasing his depression. Sibyl was up. He heard no sound. Perhaps she was already in the pottery. It was a warm morning, muggy. He showered and put on shorts and went downstairs, feeling stale and lethargic. Sibyl had left the breakfast things and a note : 'Don't forget today, gone pick up flowers and the Ramsays (their car on the blink), don't forget grass, darling, cats fed, I told you the Spensers dinner tonight, didn't I? – love and kisses, Sibyl.'

Edward knew nothing of any of it. His smile was grim. He made some tea and toast. It was twenty after ten. Did Sibyl really expect him to go out there and beat down the long wet grass? The rain was still holding off but the grass and ground were so thoroughly soaked they could take weeks to dry out. The Ramsays were Lionel and Penny, both in their twenties, both on the buses; they came only for certain meetings. Expect him to monitor the barbecue and start a headache in its smoke and the bedlam of a bunch of do-gooders filling up a Sunday? It hadn't penetrated, Sibyl couldn't get it through her head; on top of yesterday's wear and tear she thought him ripe for more, with the Spensers piled on top.

Edward left the breakfast things, went out and got in his car. He drove aimlessly, his one thought to escape Sibyl's tyranny. At the same time he wanted to shake off the confusion of disappointment and anger, emotions he knew were stultifying. He felt sure that in a tranquil, benign atmosphere he could write the script he wanted to write, the script Lindsay wanted. Just sort things out in his head so he'd calm down, and then calmly make Sibyl see. This bombshell today – Sibyl's total disregard for him and his wants, for his precious time, the failure even to warn him – he'd make the catalyst for change.

Angry horns and shouted curses brought him back to where he was: headed south on the Hume Highway. It was no place to think, caught in the Sydney-Melbourne two-way traffic augmented by Sunday drivers. At the cross roads Edward turned off towards Campbelltown and Macquarie Fields. He took a little side road and stopped.

After a blank few moments he knew what he wanted to do. He got out and locked the car, then set off at a trot. He had on rope-soled espadrilles which weren't exactly right, but his muscles told him how much he needed the exercise. The day was too muggy, the sun too hot through broken low dark clouds that imprisoned the earth in humidity. Man was impurifying the atmosphere. The young people of his film had the solution, with their beautiful son, all three at the peak of their idealistic, exuberant youth — say the mid-twenties — in a landscape far removed from this flattish district he jogged through. Theirs was beautiful, varied, the whole earth somehow telescoped. And rife with dangers. Father and son saw the dangers, explaining them to the mother so that she too became alarmed. Their warnings started a dramatic movement of the people that no machinations by governments or business combines could hope to halt. The heroic and visionary father who had Edward's face conquered all hazards with incredible strength and resilience of mind and body. He saw all problems, consulted with deferential experts, proposed remedies or counteractions designed to restore and ensure ecological stability. Salvation was implicit in theme and action: under the hero's leadership the earth would no longer be a despoiled battleground but a heaven yielding its riches to a reformed humanity. The son went everywhere with the father, his echo in face and ideas. The mother shared their nobility and tended their needs.

Edward stopped and leaned against a fence. Sweat drenched him. He was in a lane between two fields with no memory of getting there. He smiled at himself. One of his crazy daydreams. What baloney! He could hear Lindsay: Christ, old boy, cut the bloody crap and start thinking. Mud had ruined his espadrilles, spattered his legs. He was panting too much.

The mother had Sibyl's face. It was Sibyl's face had ended his dreaming. He knew it was the face he loved, that the stifled feeling he'd just got about it would go once he'd made her see. She'd be in the thick of things now: spilled drinks, overrun ashtrays, mess round the barbecue, quarrelling children, affronted cats, headachey shouts. They'd bring their own chops and sausages, it was *de rigueur* for barbecue meetings, and Nance would have brought a gift of heavy delicacies. He imagined the mess there'd still be when he got back. She'd leave it all for him instead of tending his needs. He steeled his heart against her.

He had a miserable lunch around three o'clock at a rotten little plastic café. On the way back he passed a nursery and thought of his rosemary but it was too much trouble.

He got home just after five. It seemed an eternity since he'd left that morning. The house was silent. The smell of the barbecue hung about but all other traces were gone. He went to the outside loo and then to the kitchen. It was all cleaned up. In the living-room too, even the ashtrays. Edward felt a pang. Then he remembered it should be Sibyl feeling pangs, a whole lot of pangs.

Sibyl was on her bed looking tired and unhappy. She looked at him then turned her back to him. Edward went for a shower.

It should all be so simple, not this conflict. Sibyl was selfish the way Lindsay was, expecting Edward to fit his life to her whims and timetables. He had to make a stand now before it was too late. Lindsay's thing had made it imperative.

When he got back to the bedroom Sibyl was sitting on the side of her bed with a long face. Edward put on cotton pants and a skivvy. In the glass he saw her watching him.

'You're not coming to the Spensers'?' she asked.

'No.'

'All right.'

'I'll ring and tell them why.'

'It doesn't matter.' She got up. Then in a thoughtful voice she said, 'Lindsay didn't turn up on Friday, did he?'

Edward stared at her and felt anger rising. 'What's that got to do with the price of fish?'

'A lot, it seems. You came home in a rage and you've kept it all week-end.'

'Even if it were true what's the difference?' Edward said in his quiet voice. 'I've had no week-end, have I?

Your parents all day yesterday and today's bedlam sprung
as an afterthought.'

'I'm sorry about that,' Sibyl said.

'You're always sorry.'

'I really am, but you're getting away from the point —
I just don't think you should build any hopes on Lindsay.'

'The point is leave Lindsay alone, leave me alone,
leave my free time alone.'

Despite the mildness of his voice Sibyl had an alarmed
look. It hadn't been what he'd meant to say; he'd meant
to reason with her as an ally, make her see that his needs
were just as pressing and far more personal to both of
them than those of Moreton Bay figs and single mothers.
It was Sibyl's fault for introducing the irrelevancy of
Lindsay. Edward saw too late that he should have filled
in Lindsay's time on Friday and come home when expected,
and smiling.

Sibyl was leaving the bedroom. Edward said, 'Shouldn't
you be a bit busier on your pots?'

Sibyl just kept going. She was really upset, he could tell
by that level voice she sometimes used to underscore her
seriousness. Well, so was he. Just because he'd played
along all this time she thought him a milksop to push
around as she liked.

Edward went downstairs and looked up the Spensers'
number. Julie answered. He made his apologies. 'I won't
be terribly missed, will I?' He imagined Julie's schooled
face, and smiled. 'Not at all,' Julie said with cool ambiguity.

CHAPTER VII

'That's fine, old boy, you're doing fine. Keep it up and
it's in the bag.'

Edward was jubilant. He'd had the feeling Lindsay

wasn't even listening, perched hunched on Edward's desk with a cigarette. He'd plunged right in when Lindsay asked what he had ideas-wise. He said they had to bring industry in, because industry was there, wasn't it, with enormous effect on environments, and the relationship between organisms and their environments was what ecology was all about. It would be both absurd and dishonest to ignore industry, Edward said, and by industry he meant the whole bag – mining, manufacture, armaments, processing, transport, you name it – because audiences knew a thing or two these days and knew when they were being got at. They wouldn't stand for a shirking of the truth.

Then Lindsay said, 'Anything from Sibyl?'

'There will be,' Edward said quickly, 'soon as we find time. She's extra busy just now, got a ceramics exhibition next June.' He felt proud saying it.

'Good show,' Lindsay said. 'It's just the sooner we get something down the better.'

'I couldn't agree more,' Edward said, 'how about you, done any thinking?'

'Some.' Lindsay darted a look at him. 'Only just remember this is your exercise, old boy, it's you wants to learn the bloody ropes.'

'I know, don't think I'm not grateful – for these too, they'll be very useful.'

He'd already thanked Lindsay for bringing two old film scripts. It was decent of Lindsay to remember. He hadn't mentioned the twenty he'd borrowed but that wasn't important. He'd been only a quarter of an hour late this time and Edward hadn't filled even one sheet of his notepad with faces which had Sibyl's bobbed hair and stringy neck.

'I mean, old boy, you had a project – get anything done on that?'

Edward felt his face flush. He couldn't tell Lindsay about his upwards-and-outwards young marrieds. Lindsay would laugh his head off. If only Edward had a hint of what Lindsay had in mind. Lindsay was really corny — this trilogy he was working on was about divorce wrecking people's lives, drivel from three different angles — and Edward felt sure Lindsay's fictional family was Mum, Dad and the kids. Yet he'd laugh his derisive laugh at Edward's pair, or trio, counting the son. So far the session had gone well and Edward didn't want it spoiled.

'I'm toying with a family,' he said in a careful voice.

'Great,' Lindsay said, 'bang-on. Nothing like a family to get the suckers in — Christ, old boy, *people need people,* call it what you like, married or not it beats the bloody loneliness, you don't get suburbanites identifying with bloody hermits.'

Encouraged by Lindsay's depth of feeling, Edward said, 'A man and a woman, young, enthusiastic. They have the power to inspire. And a son.'

'Toddler?'

'I thought older.'

He didn't like Lindsay's crooked smile, but Lindsay said, 'Sounds great, old boy. Start working it out from there.'

They tossed it around a bit more. Edward kept watch on Lindsay's face for any sign of derision. They left the office together. Only the cleaners about. Lindsay was going home to work. Edward drove in the happy knowledge that Lindsay liked his family : himself and Sibyl and their beautiful grave-faced son; Sibyl sweet, malleable, considerate; himself successful, creative, benevolent; the son, young Edward, noble and wise beyond his years; the house they lived in clean and spacious, a base for their regenerating programme, alive with music and books.

He saw the red-orange glow and Sibyl's station wagon. The rain that had been building all day started its pelting as he drove into the garage. He wished his room were finished so he could study Lindsay's old scripts. His right foot sank into soft mud as he tried to dodge the rain.

Sibyl was waiting. She'd heard the car. Her arms came round him as soon as he got inside. 'Darling, I'm sorry, I'm quite *ill* with being sorry.'

He held her close. They'd had words this morning about the week-end. When it had seemed finished Edward had said that with her exhibition and his film something must go by the board and it would have to be her public pursuits that filled both time and the house with people. The complacent selfishness of her reply had staggered him : 'It's okay, darling, I'm free all this week for the pottery.' 'But I'm not, am I?' He'd got up from the table. 'You've swiped all *my* free time.' He'd left for the office then because he couldn't bear to be near her another moment.

'Tired, sugar?' Sibyl asked now in a soft voice.

'I'm all right.' He wouldn't tell her about Lindsay's enthusiasm, but it was this that flooded him with tenderness. 'Been working?'

She nodded. He was still holding her. 'Very good day, I'll do some firing this week.' Then she looked into his eyes. 'Is now all right for the marvellous news, darling?'

'Sure,' Edward said with indulgence, 'after dinner, eh?' He'd forgotten the news she'd been bursting with Saturday night.

So after dinner they sat in the living-room and Sibyl started. 'Why don't we have a holiday house, darling?'

Edward was instantly wary. He knew her roundabout way of coming at things.

'Well – do we need one?' A holiday house was the last thing on his agenda, even if they could afford it.

'But wouldn't you love to *get away* sometimes?'

Edward smiled. 'Isn't that why we live out here, because it's *away*?'

'Oh Eddie, you *know* what I mean, I mean a *complete*

change, just to relax *completely,* week-ends and holidays.'

'It's hardly the time, is it, both of us so busy?'

Sibyl laughed, a self-satisfied laugh that seemed to crow over him, Edward thought. 'There's not a *thing* to worry about, sugar, Daddy's come good with the land.'

'You mean – given you some?'

'Us some, down near them, not far from our little church.'

Edward was furious. With Daddy, his land, his church, and with Sibyl. He was faced with a *fait accompli* that only required a building on it. He sat in the middle of Sibyl's frills, hating them.

'Aren't you *excited*?'

'Well, I suppose if the land's ours we're stuck with it, but that's as far as it goes, I can't afford to build, even a shack would cost the earth these days.'

Sibyl laughed again, the same laugh. 'Actually, darling, there *is* a house, the parents aren't *that* silly, it's only fibro but it's only holidays.'

Edward froze with anger and shame. Anger because it was all behind his back, because Sibyl got her own way always; shame at Daddy's patronizing handouts. He got up and went to the window, just to be doing something. The curtains repelled him. 'Why didn't he tell both of us, why only you?'

'Gosh, darling, who *cares*?'

'Obviously I do.'

There was a silence, then Sibyl said in a changed voice, 'Anyone else'd be *thrilled.*'

Edward walked about the room, stepping over the fringes of the rugs he hated. 'If I wanted a holiday house that would be the last place I'd choose.'

'That's silly.'

Edward's voice was low and intense. 'I just don't want to be bothered about it, I'm working, concentrating, it's not easy working all day and writing a film in between, I don't want extraneous things interfering, I made that clear this morning.' Today's thing with Lindsay was already marred. Instead this stifling pressure.

'I just simply don't understand,' Sibyl said.

'No, you don't. A pity.'

'I mean, Lindsay doesn't even *like* you.'

Edward smiled at her simplicity.

'You know what I think, darling?' Sibyl said.

'You've just told me.'

'I don't think it's snippets from me he's after – except of course he'd grab at simply *anything* – I think he's just stringing you along to keep you quiet, I mean he thinks you're *envious*, I mean he must *see* it, darling – '

'What a bitch you are.'

Sibyl looked horrified and upset. 'Don't say that. *I* don't think you're envious, I just mean Lindsay likes to *think* you are. *Do* sit down, darling.'

Edward said stuffily, 'Lindsay and I can manage without your amateur psychology.'

Sibyl sighed. She got out her third cigarette. 'You won't *see*, will you? You've never even *done* any writing so why on earth would Lindsay suddenly think you're an *expert*?'

If he'd been another sort of man he could have hit her then. He felt intolerably squeezed between the pleasure Lindsay's thing gave him and the pain Sibyl made out of it. His mind sought the physical escape he longed for : his room. Tomorrow Forshaw would be finished and the end of the week would see the room almost his.

He said, 'I suppose there are title deeds.'

'Of course,' Sibyl said in a cloud of smoke.

'I suppose I can see them.'

'Oh, what does it *matter*? Just because it's in my name doesn't mean it's any less *ours*.'

Rage boiled up inside Edward, and it was odd to hear the mildness of his objection. 'But it's not ours, is it?'

'Oh Eddie darling, you know what Daddy's like.' About

her, she meant: besotted. 'It's so *unimportant*, sugar, it's *ours* just the same.'

Edward left the living-room. He went outside to his herbs. The rain had eased to a dreary drizzle. Did Sibyl think she'd got away with it by attacking him and Lindsay? He saw them there at the holiday house, a depressing lop-sided shack, Daddy telling him the right way to do things, Daddy around all day, telling him how to grow his herbs, telling him the grass was too short, too long, saw the flammable house on fire and himself too late to rescue poor Sibyl, saw Daddy rush in too late, unable to escape the fire with his poor leg, Mummy too late for everything. Lindsay's thing needed a fire. In the summer. The Australian summer with a bushfire razing houses in its path. Poor Sibyl dead in the fire. Fire was a factor in the ecological process. He'd bet Lindsay hadn't thought of that.

Sibyl's voice said, 'Don't sulk, darling.' She stood with an umbrella beyond the castor oil tree. 'Come inside, you'll get wet.'

Edward followed her in, watched her fold the umbrella and stand it by the door, then followed her into the living-room. He said in his neutral voice, 'I'm just like one of your pots.'

Sibyl smiled and nestled against him. 'Silly darling.' Holding him close she tilted her head back to look at him. 'Maybe a teeny bit potty sometimes, but the darlingest man in the *world*.'

'Why'd you marry me, someone to clean up after your meetings?'

He watched the smile drain from her face, felt her arms drop away. While she stared at him he thought: that's good – the smile drained from her face – I might use that in Lindsay's thing. Only trouble was, there wasn't a face in Lindsay's thing the smile could drain from – unless he put one there. Lindsay's fictional family wouldn't have draining smiles, theirs would be toothpaste smiles fixed through all adversity.

'I really thought you'd be *thrilled* about the holiday place,' Sibyl said, back in her armchair, a cigarette going.

'So I am.' Lindsay's thing was dull, it needed true humanity, real people to bring it alive, acne and abortions, faces smiles drained from. Or lighted up, for that matter. Started up in. He felt one start in his own face.

'What's the joke?' Sibyl said.

'Nothing.'

'You look so secretive sometimes.'

'Just thinking.' He smiled at her. 'Like me to do the dishes?'

Sibyl looked happy again, and somehow relieved. 'No, darling, you just relax, the dishes is my job.'

'The dishes are,' Edward said.

'So they are.' She laughed and went.

He watched the late news but there was nothing strictly ecological. Yet couldn't the whole string of disasters that passed for news be termed ecological? Man was an organism and the earth he fought over was his environment. Man and woman : himself and Sibyl.

That night Sibyl came to his bed. He expected it; it was the pattern when Sibyl got her own way. Her victories were inevitable, the holiday house a foregone conclusion, time in her pottery taken for granted whatever else was left undone. She was so sweet, so selfishly loving him to distraction. Edward felt magnanimous towards her; Sibyl just didn't comprehend the plane he was on with Lindsay. He couldn't blame her, a lack was hardly a fault.

It was nice in bed with the wind outside blowing the rain against the windows. Sibyl was mad for his crinkly hair and the tiny curls it ended in. They made wonderful, exhausting love.

CHAPTER VIII

There was another session in Edward's office and a couple of disastrous lunch-hour meetings in pubs, then one night Edward took Lindsay home to Fernydale. He knew Sibyl was going to a meeting, he'd made a point of asking. He didn't tell Lindsay Sibyl would be out because he half-suspected Lindsay's ready agreement was precisely because he wanted to pump Sibyl for anything she knew worth knowing.

The house was passably neat from Edward's last lot of housework. It hadn't rained in the last few days and the wilderness they lived in, always depressing, was a shade less so in the dry. After dinner they'd go up to Edward's room and it would go on for stimulating hours. He had something down on paper at last and Lindsay wanted to see it.

Lindsay drank whisky and pried uninvited into the downstairs rooms while Edward made a salad and grilled the steak. If Lindsay expected wine – he might even ask for it – Edward was going to talk him out of it, because Lindsay grew more sardonic, and often unpleasant, the more he drank. A choice of mustards, three cheeses and crackers.

They'd just sat down to it in the kitchen when Sibyl came in. Edward's dismay was acute.

Lindsay got up. 'Hello there, Sibyl, lovely to see you.'

'Don't get up,' Sibyl said, '*do* sit down and get on with it.'

But Lindsay took her hand and bent to kiss it. Sibyl withdrew the hand quickly.

Lindsay said with a grin at Edward, 'I think you've rather taken the wind out of the old boy's sails.'

Sibyl gave him a cool look and then transferred it to

Edward. '*Do* go on with your dinner, both of you, I'm absolutely *stuffed* with sandwiches and cake.'

'What time's your meeting?' Edward said. He felt choked, suffocated; a mouthful of food would choke him.

'That was *it,* it's *over.*' Sibyl got a drink of water at the sink. 'We're throwing it right back in the council's lap.'

'Something environmental?' Lindsay asked in an innocent voice.

'Just an old house we're saving.' Sibyl went to the door. 'Don't mind if I vanish, do you? – I'm absolutely *dead.*'

'We're going to work,' Edward said.

After she'd gone the silence went on too long. Edward felt betrayed. He'd never seen Sibyl like that; once or twice unhappy but never so withdrawn. Her distaste for Lindsay was obvious. Had Lindsay seen it? What a pig Lindsay was, eating. The steak was tasteless, the flavour gone from everything. Lindsay got up and got another whisky, neat. Sitting down he said, 'Sibyl's not being much help, is she, old boy? It comes over loud and bloody clear.'

'She's got so much on her plate,' Edward said.

Lindsay pushed his aside. He stared unsmiling at the cheeses. Edward bit his lip and got up to put the percolator on. He didn't know what to say; he should be able to toss off some lighthearted comment, as Lindsay would.

'Bloody funny,' Lindsay said, 'I'd have thought wild enthusiasm.'

'She's tired,' Edward said, 'just right now and all the time, she works very hard, there's her show on top of everything else.'

He put mugs on the tray and got out cream and sugar. He'd spoken with too much intensity. He heard Lindsay behind him at the whisky again.

They took the coffee upstairs but Edward knew the bottom had fallen out of the evening. Lindsay had come in Edward's car so Edward would have to drive him home. He'd looked forward to it, now it loomed as a tiring

chore. Lindsay could get a taxi but he'd expect Edward
to drive him, he'd enjoy making Edward drive him.

Upstairs was utter silence. Sibyl lying low. Edward put
the tray down to unlock his door while Lindsay leaned
on the wall looking morose. Edward had longed for this
moment : his room revealed to Lindsay. But Lindsay saw
nothing, just staggered in and fell into the armchair.
Edward carried the tray to his desk, plugged in the percolator and poured. Lindsay waved his hand at the mug
of coffee so Edward put it beside the armchair on the
floor.

Lindsay's eyes were shut. Edward sat at his desk and
began reading through the few pages of script he'd done.
It seemed to him dreadful stuff, silly, meaningless. Lindsay
would call it a pile of bloody rubbish. Edward squeezed
his hands hard together. It was Sibyl's fault for bursting
in when she said she'd be out. Or was it Lindsay's fault?
Something always occurred to foul things up with Lindsay.
Perhaps it was something about Lindsay himself.

Lindsay's voice made him jump. 'I'm all washed up, old
boy, better push off.' He had his twist of smile and was
bleary-eyed.

'Too much whisky,' Edward said. 'Like me to drive you
home?'

'Like you to ring me a taxi. Like to take your stuff.'

Edward hesitated, then thought why not? How else
were they to get anywhere with the film? Downstairs he
watched Lindsay stuff the foolscap pages into his briefcase.
Lindsay said he'd phone and went off in the taxi.

Edward went up to his room again and locked himself
in. At least the room had gone swimmingly. No curtains
yet, but they'd be coming soon. The lighting was splendid,
indirect, just right, with an angled lamp on his desk. It
was spotless, uncluttered, such a contrast to the rest of the
house. He loved the charcoal carpet. The furniture fitted as
he'd known it would. Apart from the view and location,

he thought his room superior to Lindsay's workroom. It was more solid, looked more permanent. Last time he was at Lindsay's, over two years ago, Edward thought the whole place, including the room where Lindsay worked, had a fly-by-night look. Lindsay went in for coloured hard plastic shapes a lot, expensive and cluttery, and lots of enormous floor cushions. Edward's room had serenity.

He picked up Lindsay's untouched coffee, then sat at his desk. He wished now he'd typed the pages of script so he had a copy. Lindsay might lose the only copy. He must get used to working on the typewriter, the way Lindsay did. It was crazy not to use it now that he'd bought it. There was something more satisfying to Edward in pen and paper. His small scriptlike writing was neat, as legible as typewritten stuff. He used a ruler to underline headings and proper names, always with two red lines. Edward had to be neat and precise in order to think clearly. The room was essential to it. He could never order thought in Sibyl's sloppy atmosphere.

He tried to remember the pages he'd given Lindsay to read, and couldn't. It embarrassed him to think of Lindsay reading them. He still had Lindsay's old film scripts and pulled one towards him. It made him remember the visuals he'd used: establishing the Australian scene in all its variety of rivers, lakes, mountains, plains, coastline, desert, forests. Then the mother and son. Sibyl and young Edward. He'd given them other names but they always appeared to him as Sibyl and a virile young version of himself. No one would ever know so why should he feel constrained about it? And about himself, the father, not yet on paper, the avenging angel who put their world to rights?

He kept expecting Sibyl to knock. He got up and dusted his books, taking each separately from the shelves and piling them on his desk. He'd had a whole lot of books sent out, every kind of reference book and everything he could find on ecological subjects. Plus some others picked at random because they gave him a feeling of solidity – Shakespeare, Herodotus, Cervantes, Thomas Mann, Dostoevski, stuff like that. He'd like the time to read them all, the time and peace. Also he had a pile of brand-new dusters, and a big feather duster he liked flicking around.

It was past midnight by the time he was done. Sibyl hadn't knocked. That meant she'd gone to bed in a pet because he'd brought Lindsay home without telling her. She'd think it was behind her back, but Edward was sure he hadn't meant it that way.

Stealthily, so he wouldn't wake her, Edward crept to the bathroom and had a shower. Then he went in silence to the bedroom. Sibyl's ragged breathing told him she was asleep. The noise grated on him. In the pale dark of the night he hated the room, the mess on the dressing-table, Sibyl's clothes chucked about, a shoe he almost tripped over. Edward took the blanket from his bed, cautiously so she wouldn't wake. He took it to his room and locked the door.

He lay on the divan. He liked the way it was, flat and unyielding. He threw the blanket over his lower half and pushed off all the cushions but one. The windows were open and there were a few stars. It was nice in here. Why not more often? Sibyl might be hurt. It was good to enjoy solitariness again. He remembered how he'd loved the novelty of sharing a bedroom with Sibyl, having Sibyl all over it. But wasn't that all it had been: a novelty? He didn't love her less. It was just the shambles that crowded in, crowding him out. He couldn't any longer shut his eyes to it. And her outside interests that made him feel superfluous. It was a relief to have somewhere free of her mess. And her laughter.

Then working on Lindsay's thing wasn't all at the desk. He had to think things out, toss them around, and for that he needed peace. Peace meant solitude. Now that he had both there was time to wonder what work Lindsay had done on the script. Lindsay set him little projects and mostly looked dubious at anything Edward came up with, but what did Lindsay come up with? At the back of Edward's mind the suspicion haunted him, the suspicion that Sibyl might be right, or partly right, that a professional like Lindsay would never turn to Edward for collaboration. And yet it didn't make sense. As for his envy of Lindsay, Sibyl was quite wrong there, because Edward had swallowed it in his anxiety to retain Lindsay's friendship. When had he ever pestered Lindsay? Once or twice, perhaps, he'd told Lindsay he ought to value his health more, value his talent more. He liked the remaining motive: Lindsay had started on the idea and got stuck, being already up to his ears on his trilogy. He'd gone stale, dried up, perhaps cast about in vain for a springboard into the subject. Lindsay's thing needed a fresh outlook, and that Lindsay believed it could come from Edward was the stuff dreams are made of.

Suddenly, Edward believed the pages of script he'd given Lindsay to read were good, at any rate a good basis. He remembered something ecological Sibyl had said once: 'Look at the *giraffe,* darling, it's tall like that for *eating.*' He smiled. She meant its neck had developed to enable it to eat high foliage. *Look at the Giraffe.* Anything in that as a title? Symbolic of the whole thing? Sibyl and her absorbing interests. The film Sibyl was very nearly the real Sibyl, just a whole lot tidier, more considerate, not selfish, not ageing, not slovenly, never doubting her husband's superior abilities.

He was half-asleep. At the happy stage when his film had its own momentum.

A knocking woke him. There was a blank suspended moment. Then Sibyl's voice.

'You in there, Eddie? It's *late.*'

Edward sat up and swung his legs round. He was shivery. Sibyl hadn't seen his room yet.

'*Eddie.*'

It might as well be now. Edward went to the door and opened it.

'You're *naked.*'

Edward smiled drowsily. 'You've seen me a million times, but what about this?' He waved at the room. 'Like it?'

'Yes, darling, I've seen it, *do* hurry up, you'll be late, and bring the coffee things.'

'How seen it?'

'Gosh, *I* don't know, it was open one day I suppose, poached with bacon?'

'Anything you like.' Edward felt last night's betrayal back again, compounded now.

When he got downstairs Sibyl said, 'Beautiful timing, done to a turn – *no*, pussy, you had the rind.'

The cat and Edward watched her slide the eggs out. 'I expected you to be out last night, you implied it,' Edward said, 'I wouldn't have brought Lindsay here if I'd known you'd be home so early.'

'Why on earth didn't you *say*?'

'I didn't want an argument.'

'Eat your breakfast, darling. I'd have made a *point* of being out if I'd known.'

Edward didn't move.

'*Do* sit down, Eddie, it's all so *silly.*'

'Any sillier than your meetings and all your stodgy pots?'

After a pause Sibyl said, 'I'd no idea it meant so much to you.'

'No.' Then as if to himself he added, 'It's your life that counts, so long as nothing interferes with that it's all that matters.'

Sibyl sat down and got out a Weetabix. 'Aren't you going to eat your breakfast?'

'I'm not hungry.' Edward stared through the greyish

curtains at the darker sky. It was going to rain again.

'You never raise your voice, even angry.' Hers was soft.

He turned to her. 'I'm not angry.'

'Sleeping there – not that I mind, only if you were angry.'

'I didn't want to disturb you.'

'I'm sorry, darling – if I'd known – I can see now why you felt disappointed – you've every right to lunge out.' She looked close to tears.

Edward went to her, touched her hair, then bent and kissed it.

Sibyl jumped up and hugged him. 'Oh Eddie, you *are* a darling.'

'Yes.'

'I'm a selfish *pig.*'

'Yes.'

Sibyl laughed: his laugh. The private, loving, confiding laugh he'd loved from the first. I've lived this moment before, he thought. Then he knew it was his daydream: Sibyl thinking only of him, not all the time of them. This reality was almost as good as the dream, but not quite. In the dream she didn't hamper his work, in the dream she encouraged and admired. She didn't call him Eddie in the dream. He detested Eddie as much as he hated sugar.

To please Sibyl he ate the cooling eggs and bacon. Sibyl brought the teapot. 'You're going to be late.'

'It won't hurt for once.'

'Darling, I was thinking,' she sat down and watched his face, 'wouldn't you like Christmas away?'

'I don't like Christmas anywhere.'

'No, but I mean – well don't let's go into *that* seeing we're stuck with it – I mean our holiday house.'

'No.'

'Oh *Eddie*! The parents want us down there anyway, so I thought you'd like it better not right in their laps, in our *own place*.' She blew smoke so that Edward had to dodge.

'No, darling.'

'But why *not*?'

'I don't like it there, least of all in summer. Then there's the film,' he remembered a phrase of Lindsay's, 'I'll need to keep my head down on that. And three, I'd never go to a shack I hadn't seen, how do we know what – ?'

'But it's *furnished*, Mummy's put her old fridge in and – '

'Sagging mattresses, cobwebs, grimy fingerprints, a broken-down old fridge – '

'It's *not* broken-down, it's a good one.'

'No, darling, perhaps a bit later, March, April, I could get my holidays – there'd be less people then. Four, your exhibition.'

'What's that got to do with it? I'll have it ready in time.'

'Lucky you.'

'The parents' place, then?' His face answered her. 'Not even just three days?'

Edward drank the last of his tea.

'Just two?'

Edward got up.

'Well, there's time to change your mind,' Sibyl said, 'it's only 19th of November.'

Edward bent over and kissed her cheek. 'I'm off now.'

'Oh darling,' she called from the table, 'I've got a meeting tonight'll go on for simply *hours*, ZPG and world food shortages, there's a visiting American, so if you want to bring Lindsay – ?'

'Not tonight. 'Bye.' He started towards the garage.

Sibyl called from the back door. 'How about come to the meeting, sugar? We could snatch a bite before it starts.'

Edward shook his head and smiled and went into the garage. Sibyl followed him. 'Don't you care at *all* about international horrors?'

'Yes, I care about lots of things.' He turned the ignition. 'Don't drive too fast,' Sibyl said. She blew a kiss as he passed.

I care about us, Edward thought, Sibyl and me. I care about privacy and peace and solitude, and never again loneliness. And that old man – no, he's not old, he just looks old – ransacking a litter bin, poor enough to grab at Mummy's V-neck steel-grey sleeveless pullover – tomorrow I'll bring it and shove it in there. And the rain starting again. And about those children going to school. This unrestricted urban mess. I care about international horrors. And little local horrors. And domestic horrors. Most of all I care about succeeding with Lindsay's thing.

Lindsay had said he'd phone. Without really expecting it that day Edward thought every ring might be Lindsay. There was no point in jotting down random notes until he got Lindsay's go-ahead. But that didn't stop the film in his head unrolling its ideal world. He was expert at his job, safe in it, and Edward knew he was the only staff member Mr Strachan smiled at. Mr Wykeham smiled at no one so didn't count. The film and Edward's work went ahead together.

Just after four-thirty Lindsay breezed into the office. A smiling Miss Goldman brought him; Lindsay must have joked with her. Miss Goldman had the switchboard at the front desk.

'Can't stop, old boy, came into town without a bloody bean, would you believe it? Can you manage a tenner?'

Edward got out his wallet.

'That's all this one rates,' Lindsay said with the twist of his lips, taking the note and stuffing it in his pocket. 'By the way,' he was on his way out, 'read your stuff, might be able to turn it around somehow, thought of a tangent you might like a go at – lovers, cut the maternal crap, few nude scenes – kick it around and I'll be in touch.' He poked his head back round the door and slapped his pocket. 'Haven't forgotten the other, old boy, makes thirty, doesn't it?' A hand wave and he was gone.

I care about trusting Lindsay, Edward thought, I care terribly. A suspicion arose that he was paying Lindsay for the privilege of working on the script. If that were so why not turn the tables? If Lindsay went on borrowing without repaying there might be a lever there Edward could use. He felt ashamed for Lindsay and for his own inglorious reasoning. But there was the other anxiety: Lindsay thought him a fool who might just hit on something. Could it be true that Lindsay was humouring him, stringing him along so he could pronounce Edward hopeless, bloody hopeless, and so slide out of their friendship? Had Lindsay found another tax accountant, as good as Edward but more to his personal taste? Wasn't it time Edward grew a bit more secretive about his ideas, insist Lindsay come across with some of his own? He wanted to trust Lindsay. But Lindsay was slippery in all his dealings, he joked about it. Edward couldn't resist the suspicion that Lindsay was stealing the ideas he kept rebuffing.

Lindsay still had Edward's pages, the only copy.

Nude scenes!

CHAPTER IX

Lindsay phoned next morning. Was Monday convenient for Edward in his office after hours? He sounded sober and businesslike, as though speaking to a partner and equal. Edward said that was fine, matching his voice to Lindsay's, not revealing his delight and relief. During his lunch hour, in celebration, he went to a store with a big gardening section and bought a flourishing rosemary.

Sibyl was out when he got home. Edward was glad. It meant he could smile, and hum a tune, or turn a cart-

wheel if he wanted to, without her eyes, cynical or commiserating, even if she said nothing. The thing with
Lindsay grew fragile in Sibyl's presence; somehow she
made him feel on guard. A note on the kitchen table
said she'd be late and was sorry she'd forgotten to tell
him and roast beef in the oven in foil with baked pumpkin
and salad in the fridge and turn the oven off and she'd
fed the cats.

Edward got a gin and tonic and took it outside to
where he'd left the rosemary. He dug a hole and transferred the plant, careful to keep its soil intact. He was sure
this one would live; something as healthy couldn't possibly
die. The parsley was done for, yellowed and shrivelling,
but he smiled at the riotous mint and lifted his glass to it.
The rain had kept off since yesterday afternoon and there
were a few stars. It struck Edward then that he might see
the southern cross from his room with a bit of craning.
Tonight he'd look for it.

While he was getting a fresh drink he remembered the
news at seven. He switched it on ready. He finished his
drink and got another. Lindsay drank, coped with it.
Parliamentary wrangles, cricket, South-East Asia, missing
bushwalkers, overseas air crash killing 141, supermarkets'
discount war, strikes looming in beer, mail and transport.
None of it strictly ecological, but in the wider sense wasn't
it all? The entire earth, all its people and their activities?
His mind was like a searchlight on the whole earth, on the
universe. He was on his third drink, an indulgence to
celebrate success, because success had been in Lindsay's
voice this morning. It seemed so clear how the film should
be: a searchlight on a group of people – his family trio,
say – themselves thrashing out how to encompass in a film
the enormous pressing problem of maintaining ecological
sanity. No, not maintaining: enforcing. It was so clear,
as if in a searchlight's beam. Searchlight. It was a good
word. *Searchlight*, by Edward Piper. Smiling, Edward

switched off the TV and went to the kitchen.

Sibyl's succulent beef reminded him of Mummy, a depressing thought that made him remember the pullover. He went up at once and fished it out and folded it into his briefcase. No point in telling Sibyl, she'd only laugh anyway – or perhaps she wouldn't.

He finished his meal with a sliver of Edam, put the food away and added his used things to the unwashed stack in the dishwasher. Then he went up to his room, taking the ice bucket, gin and tonic.

He didn't mean to get drunk – he never had – he meant only to prolong the searchlight of his thinking. He made notes on his new ideas. He'd intended to wait for Lindsay's opinion on what he'd already done but creativeness wouldn't be stifled. He watched his ideas flow. He couldn't write fast enough. He filled page after page of his notepad.

And then the truth struck him. His searchlight revealed the whole idea as absurd. Ecology couldn't be squashed into an hour, not even into two or three. There were scientists who'd been studying small areas of the Great Barrier Reef for years, and they were still just on the fringes of knowing a fraction. And that was only the Reef, just one dot in the whole world pattern, even in the Australian continental pattern. In a way he was back to his first suggestion to Lindsay: start with one plant. It was Lindsay with his fictional family who'd introduced absurdity. Or was it commercialism? Lindsay thought commercially. Edward saw a film could be made on an aspect of ecology, the basic equation, but an understanding of ecology *in toto* was a long educational process they wouldn't live to see. Lindsay didn't have a clue, he didn't know what ecology was. Lindsay's idea was a dead duck. The conclusion made Edward feel superior, but to show it would be fatal. The thing was to make Lindsay see.

Edward sat back with a fresh drink. He felt sure he

could make Lindsay see.

'You in there, sugar?'

Edward frowned, got up and opened the door.

'*Gosh,* on the grog?' She laughed, then said, 'Guess what?' She was hugging a cat.

Edward smiled.

'I got my resolution passed by eight votes to six – isn't that *marvellous?*'

'Wonderful, darling.' He didn't ask what it was.

'Had a good firing day, too – coming to bed?'

'There in a minute.'

Edward was happy too. His was a different happiness, deeper, an inner intellectual contentment not depending on exclamations and outcries.

'*Gosh,* darling, *not* in the *bedroom.*' Sibyl made a face at his glass. 'You *know* I can't bear the smell of gin.'

Edward took it to the bathroom and left it there.

Over breakfast next morning he said, 'There won't be room for these things in the dishwasher.'

'Didn't you do it last night?'

'No, I didn't.' Anger flared at her presumption, he was furious with his headache. 'The whole place looks like a pigsty.'

'Hangover?' Sibyl laughed. 'Well, cheer up, today's the big clean-up day.'

'High time.'

He didn't kiss her goodbye, somehow he couldn't, and it wasn't just the hangover. He stopped at the litter bin and dropped Mummy's pullover into it, poking it down, venting his feelings on it. He'd thought of the man being there, of watching his face light up, but found after all that satisfaction lay in getting rid of the pullover.

It seemed a long wait till Monday, but he'd put the time to good use in marshalling his arguments for Lindsay. Clean up his room too, a pleasure in itself. Maybe a jogtrot Sunday if the rain was still holding off; it was mostly inland areas that were inundated by floods.

The moment he got inside he saw the clean-up day had gone for a Burton. Edward sighed.

'Hi, sugar,' Sibyl called from the kitchen.

'Be down in a minute,' Edward said.

After the bathroom he went to his room, eager to run through his notes again. They seemed a meagre lot, after all. And the room looked different; it felt different. Weren't the cushions piled in a new arrangement? The stuff on his desk in a muddle? The feeling he had was surer than the evidence. He went downstairs with anger knotting inside.

'I'd like you to leave my things alone, darling, stay out of my room.' His voice was low and firm.

'I *do*, sugar, don't I? I *have* to, you keep it locked.' So casual, so careless, not turning from the stove, prodding at something in a saucepan.

'Things have been moved about.'

Sibyl turned with a fork, smiling. 'All that gin, you just don't remember, darling.'

Edward's anger burst through the suffocating feeling. 'You said you'd clean up today.'

'I *meant* to, darling, I thought a couple of hours in the pothouse then get stuck in, but Helen Jones rang about – '

'Why don't you get a woman for God's sake? How can I work in all this mess? For that matter how can you? Cat hairs everywhere. I need things shipshape for peace of mind and – and – independence of spirit. One night I saw a cockroach in here.'

'*Gosh!*' She was mashing potatoes. 'You having a drink?'

It hadn't got through to her, or she didn't care. Edward needed a drink but he couldn't face more talk about hangovers. 'Just look around you at the kitchen,' he said, 'and the bathroom upstairs is disgusting.'

Sibyl sighed. 'Poor Eddie, it's only a bit of dust. Don't let it get you *down* so. Look at Nance and the muddle *she's* always in. Jeff doesn't seem to mind.'

'I'm not Jeff.'

'Well, I mean – some people can be happy. You ready to eat?'

He wasn't ready but he sat down. Sibyl was on his nerves. The slapdashery.

On Saturday, after the shopping, he did the housework. It was useless to rail at Sibyl, she'd never change. In between the telephone Sibyl told him what a darling he was.

'I put the house to rights while you put the world to rights.'

Sibyl smiled, just as if that were the proper order of things. Edward thought another man might let bitterness grow, a man unable to adapt as he'd adapted, as he'd always swallowed all life's disappointments. At least he had Lindsay, and was another day nearer their meeting.

The phone kept on through the afternoon. Sometimes Edward answered, and around four there was yet another female for Sibyl he said hello to. Sibyl's light voice with its emphases seemed the perennial background to his housework dreaming.

'That was Diana.'

Edward was putting the finishing touches to the living-room. He nodded.

'She can't come to the party.'

'Oh. What party?'

'*Ours*, darling, for Christmas. Didn't I say? We didn't have one last year.'

'Okay,' Edward said. 'When?'

'Friday the fifth, so it won't conflict with everyone else's.'

'Fine.' He could spare an evening for Sibyl because by then he and Lindsay would have their approach planned. 'Diana Lucas?'

'Of *course*, sugar.'

Edward was aware of a total lack of interest in Sibyl's doings. It made him afraid. Sibyl was all he had – well, not quite all now he had Lindsay's thing, but with more lasting stability than Lindsay's thing. He knew she really loved him, deep down where it mattered, and it was the only certainty life held. That was wrong, he wanted creative ability as the bulwark of his life.

'Like to eat out tonight?' he said suddenly.

'*Eddie* darling, I'd *love* it.' She rushed at him with a hug.

Edward phoned around and got them in at a place he'd heard Lindsay say was good. It was pleasant to see Sibyl out of jeans or shorts, in a long pink thing cleverly concealing her stringy neck and revealing the good points. They enjoyed themselves. It seemed they'd both forsworn hobby horses for the evening. Edward told a few funny stories about Mr Wykeham, Mr Strachan's weird old junior partner who never smiled, and Sibyl said he was a *marvellous* raconteur when he wanted to be. They drove home with Sibyl's head on his shoulder.

It filled in time.

On Sunday Jeff came round in the afternoon to look at Sibyl's progress, and he was the only visitor. Edward spring-cleaned his room, spinning it out, urging the day to pass. He'd meant to go for a jogtrot but lacked the impetus. Except for Jeff's brief visit the week-end had been free, yet somehow it had been just as disorganized, just as lost, as any. It was the house itself and Sibyl's aura filling it. It hung in every frill and tassel. The cats were part of it. This room that was his haven – why not move in entirely? Yesterday he'd known Sibyl would never change, and this could be the way out of a situation that might grow intolerable for both of them.

He acted at once, making up the divan from his twin bed. It would be a nuisance having to make and unmake it night and morning, but worth it. The stuff could go in the bottom drawer of the filing thing. He'd still have to use the wardrobe in the bedroom, unless he supplied a remedy.

He went downstairs. Jeff was still there, they were having a drink in the living-room. Edward joined them.

'She's doing fine,' Jeff told Edward. 'Like the new work?'

'Very much,' Edward said.

Sibyl laughed. But she didn't give him away.

'First pure sculpture she's done,' Jeff said.

They chatted a bit more about the ceramics Edward hadn't seen.

During dinner he told her about the room. 'I think a lot at night, darling, and I hate disturbing you, and if I feel like working late I don't want the worry of –'

'Gosh, darling, skip the justification. I suppose I can pop *in* sometimes, can't I, and sometimes you'll visit *me*?'

Edward laughed. Sibyl was always easygoing. But a moment later it occurred to him she ought to have minded more.

When Sibyl came up to bed he heard her high-pitched voice. *'Gosh,* isn't it *bare* – looks like a *death* in the family!'

Edward smiled and called good night.

There was the moon sliding down the sky. The curtains were coming any day now. A little real world of his own he was master in, just as in his daydream he was the superior being, a man of exquisite judgment whose ideas Lindsay accepted and Sibyl applauded; whose name topped Lindsay's, and even sometimes stood alone, among the credits of the world-acclaimed film.

CHAPTER X

About 5.15 Edward entered his office block and strode across the foyer to the lifts. They were busy at this hour bringing down the scramble of home-goers. It was unprecedented for him to leave the office during hours, but this was an unprecedented day. It was great to feel so confident. Confidence was ninety per cent of success. Look at Lindsay, always so sure of himself; Daddy too, and Sibyl. It was confidence had taken him striding through the crowds and the tinsel glitter of the retailers' Christmas, pushing through them to the select place where he'd bought the divan and bookshelves.

Going up he watched the floor numbers glow in the same sunset colour as Sibyl's light bulbs. He got out at ten and stopped off at the men's room. It was a different face he saw in the glass; the same features, hair, eyes, but relaxed. A winner's face.

They'd still had the corner unit he'd remembered and no wonder, the price it was. Imported, beautiful solid wood, stained a subtly-dim strawberry colour, with inlaid brass handles on drawers and cupboards. It would take his clothes, hanging and folded. Except for the bathroom, and of course meals, he'd be entirely self-contained. It would fit in the window corner of the divan wall, just as it was, although they'd explained in their gratified voice how easily it divided into three separate units. It would be delivered on Wednesday.

Miss Goldman passed him in the corridor with a smiling good night. Edward went on to his office. The air-conditioned atmosphere was chilling. He went to the window. Down in the street a tangle of traffic sent up fumes so powerful the air shuddered. A blue sky for once. A tiny cloud appeared and disintegrated like a brief regret. He wished Lindsay were more poetic. Maybe he was shy about it, maybe it came out on paper. It was hard to imagine Lindsay shy about anything. He hoped Lindsay wouldn't keep him waiting around today. Lindsay was always so – engaged was more the word than busy. Edward couldn't imagine how Lindsay got any writing done at all, with his non-stop social and career contacts. But according to Lindsay he did it all on his ear.

He really had something for Lindsay today: a whole new concept. If Lindsay wanted to hang on to his nude lovers, well, let him, so long as he recognized that Edward's idea was something totally different. Why not two films, their joint effort and Lindsay's?

Edward strode round the office, swinging his arms. He felt bounding with energy, just in the mood for the jogtrot he'd shied off from yesterday. He thought of his dream of the shape his life should take, with a grimace for life's reality.

The phone rang. Only Lindsay had his direct number when the switchboard was closed, not even Sibyl. Edward's hand hovered. If Lindsay were going to cry off again he wouldn't be able to bear it.

'Hello.'

'Hi, there. Look, old boy, I can't make it in there right now but how about you come out here? Can do?'

Edward held his breath. 'Fine,' he said in a carefully casual voice, 'right away.'

He didn't mind the traffic. He deferred, smiling, to scowling drivers. They had a right to scowl, caught in the old treadmill, beset by every day's fresh crop of crises. Only Edward was favoured, invited to Lindsay's unit for a writer-to-writer conference, a meeting of equals maybe lasting into the small hours. The world was superior for him, and he was superior in it. On the phone Lindsay had sounded at his most casual, and Edward knew this to mean that Lindsay was in a serious creative mood. Edward took it for granted he'd stay the night.

Going downhill to Double Bay he felt a warm rush of friendship for Lindsay. This change in his life had begun because Lindsay had turned to him, not condescendingly but out of need, so that Edward had been able to accept. All his life he'd frozen up when the ball came his way. This time his friend Lindsay had passed him the ball and Edward had caught it. For once a smile from fate.

Diana opened the door and a blast of music hit him. 'Hello, Edward, come on in. Long time. You look well.'

'Very well, thanks.' He seemed to have to shout; the whole place shook to the thunderous beat.

'How's my Sibyl?'

'Very well.' Edward smiled. He resented 'my Sibyl', he hated the noise, he loathed it that Diana was there. Perhaps she was going soon.

'The great man's in the kitchen.' Diana gestured boredly, moved in her thin little way to a yellow chair and fell into it. The same short dark hair flopping over her eyes.

Edward turned left to the kitchen because it seemed expected, holding his briefcase.

'Hi, old boy.' Lindsay grinned in a funny apron and jigged in time to the music, waving a wooden spoon. 'Bit of a domestic evening – sheds a new bloody light on the old genius, eh? Drink, old boy? Hey, Diana,' he yelled. Then to Edward, 'Relax, old boy, shove that bloody thing somewhere, you look like a bloody accountant.' He laughed as if at a joke. He had a drink going, Edward saw, and it could be his third or fourth by the look of him.

Diana leaned in the doorway.

'Get the man a drink, old girl.'

'Okay. Come on,' she said to Edward. Edward followed her. He'd seen even less of Diana than Sibyl had of Lindsay. No more than twice since that long-ago night at the theatre. The same heavy eye make-up and lipstick, dark brown eyes under the hair, white skin. Lindsay said a good dresser, but Edward hated the slinky, clinging, one-piece vermilion trouser thing she was in, flaring out at the bottoms. He didn't like Diana because she was here in Lindsay's place when he'd expected – he didn't like Diana anyway. She was a tiny girl, small bones, thin, yet with a way of moving like someone tall.

He said gin and tonic please. Diana said ugh. She had whisky, the same as Lindsay. She gave him his drink and fell again into the yellow chair. Edward felt stiff standing there with the glass and briefcase. He put the briefcase down on a pile of coffee-table books.

'Siddown,' Diana said. Edward sat down on a hard cube in purple. 'Sib's show coming along all right? She working hard?'

'Yes,' Edward said. Sibyl must have told Diana, or Lindsay had. 'How're things with you, still in the same job?' They had to shout over the music.

'Uh-huh. Suits me fine, suits the boss, why change?'

'Why indeed.' Diana was the valued secretary of the managing director of a big paper products firm.

Lindsay came prancing in like an intoxicated gnome. 'All right, old boy? Being looked after?'

Edward smiled and waved his glass, and wondered whether they saw his tension and felt sure they did. The record stopped and Diana put on another.

It went on like that: the music, Diana's boredom, Lindsay's clatter and bursts of song in the kitchen. Edward saw the dining-room ready, the table set, candles. Maybe it was Diana who was staying the night. He got up with the drink he'd barely touched and went to the kitchen. One thing was certain: he couldn't discuss the film with Diana present. Lindsay was doing several things at once. Edward watched, waiting for a moment of calm.

'They say all chefs go stark raving mad,' Lindsay said with a grin. 'I don't blame the poor buggers.'

Edward tried to sound casual. 'I guess we won't talk about the script with Diana here.'

'Just as you like, old boy,' Lindsay said carelessly, 'she'd be bored to bloody death, anyway.' He looked amused. Edward suddenly felt the insincerity Sibyl had warned him about. 'Send her out to lend a hand, old boy, will you?'

The food was good, Lindsay a good host, not as drunk as he'd appeared in the kitchen. During the meal Edward told himself his suspicion meant nothing, it was just Lindsay being Lindsay. And Diana was nothing to do with it. If Edward put all his eggs in one basket it was hardly Lindsay's fault, was it? Lindsay would call him a bloody fool. He told himself he expected too much of something that would be a minor affair to Lindsay. Diana would go soon after dinner, alone probably, knowing they'd want to talk.

Then he had the idea they were secretly laughing at him. He saw their exchange of smiles and significant looks. He felt an intangible menace in the situation. Why had Lindsay asked him to come with Diana here? And why was Diana here? The answer was simple: Lindsay had forgotten his date with Edward until the last moment. He hadn't mentioned Edward's pages of script, not even when they were alone in the kitchen.

Why couldn't he be like Lindsay: off-hand about success? In daydreams ideas flowed with a smooth brilliance. Back to earth people fouled things up. Lindsay, the job he was tied to, Sibyl. Reality was full of doubts and interruptions. He'd had the thought sometimes it would be a relief to be free of Sibyl, then he could better deal with Lindsay's manipulation of him. Match Lindsay's cunning with his own.

Their laughter reached him. 'What they call a brown study,' Lindsay said grinning.

'Sorry,' Edward smiled.

'I was just telling you, old boy, I'm having a week away, bit of peace and quiet.'

'Good idea,' Edward said, feeling empty, 'when?'

'Off next Sunday,' Lindsay said, 'back the Sunday following.'

At that moment Edward resolved to start on his new idea, then he could dazzle Lindsay with his progress when Lindsay got back. 'Sensible time to go,' he said, 'before the holiday swarms get there. Where you going?'

'Hayman. Booked to the bloody rafters over Christmas, they tell me.'

Edward knew the evening was a dead loss. He'd have liked to leave at once, with one of the easy acceptable lies a Lindsay or a Sibyl got away with. But he felt so awkward, and had to wait for the moment when they seemed to expect him to go. Plainly Diana wasn't budging. He didn't like her little bored smile.

'I'll give you a tinkle, old boy,' Lindsay said.

'Beaut grub,' Edward said, the silly words sounding false and clumsy.

The stars were out. On the drive home the clear sweep of sky above the telegraph poles seemed to hold all kinds of promise. Edward felt sad that Lindsay wasn't his sort of person, then thought how rare his sort of person, the kind he could feel in tune with, was. Then he had another thought: Diana wasn't coming to Sibyl's party because she'd be at Hayman Island with Lindsay. Well, why not? But the thought tormented him, shutting out the sky. Had Lindsay told Diana about the film? Did they laugh together about him? Lindsay hadn't mentioned the money he owed.

Going in something hit him as he reached the foot of the stairs, like a bunch of rattling snakes. Then he saw it was a bead curtain, wooden beads in Sibyl's favourite pink. Edward struck at it savagely, causing it to retaliate. He was in no mood for more of Sibyl's disguises.

'What on *earth*?' Sibyl came out of the living-room.

'Why this?' Edward asked in his reasonable voice.

'Well, it's so *pretty*, darling, Helen Jones found them, we've *all* got them.'

'All right,' Edward said, 'I'm tired, good night.'

Sibyl's voice followed him. 'Want anything, sugar?' He ignored it and went on up. 'Your curtains are there,' she yelled.

The big parcel was outside his room, the rod separate, both wrapped in the store's paper.

Sibyl was halfway up. 'They couldn't hang them, being locked out.'

'It's okay,' Edward said. He waited for her to go. She did her baffled-bonhomie shrug and went downstairs again.

Relief to be in his room. Its silence. The clear, pure, deflected light. Outside the stars, serene, floating. The notes he'd made waiting on the desk. He had a shower and came back. He opened the parcels. He'd fix them himself at the week-end. Seated at his desk he thought how strange it was that work on the script had isolated him. What he'd so longed for – to be creative – was isolating him from the two people who'd saved him from loneliness. Just now it was an effort to think of himself in relation to either. Objectively he knew Sibyl meant well, and Lindsay too. Yet Lindsay was out of reach in a different world and Sibyl wrapped up in her own concerns. Something about them made him feel cut off. It was a worse loneliness than any he'd known. He despised Sibyl's snap judgments yet felt infected by her distrust of Lindsay. It seemed to him Lindsay's intention was to steal his ideas. All he had now was his new concept and that he would never relinquish. Share perhaps on guaranteed equal terms, but never hand over holus-bolus.

He felt tired out from disappointment. He locked his notes in a drawer. Later when Sibyl tapped gently he pretended to be asleep.

The unit came on Wednesday. It was upstairs waiting outside his room. Out of the blue, Sibyl said, adding on a note of reproof it was lucky she'd been at home. Edward thought of Sibyl's countless forgettings.

'How'll you get it in?' she asked. She was stirring something pungent with herbs in a saucepan.

'Easy,' Edward said, and ran up the stairs two at a time.

'Don't be long,' Sibyl called, then followed him. 'I've a meeting tonight, sugar, so it's spaghetti.'

Edward unlocked his door. Each of the three parts of the unit was heavy, but Edward was strong. The heaviest section he 'walked' across the floor. The unit fitted snugly in the corner he'd meant it for. He wished Sibyl wouldn't watch every move. He went to the bedroom and began to transfer his clothes.

'For heaven's *sake*, Eddie, do it *later*.'

Edward continued until he'd moved everything. Sibyl had gone downstairs. When he got down to the kitchen she was dishing up and a salad was on the table.

Sibyl laughed. 'It's just like having a *lodger*.'

On Friday the rain came back and during the afternoon Lindsay rang him at the office.

'Read your stuff again.'

Edward waited, then when the silence continued said, 'Yes?' He could picture Lindsay's sardonic smile.

'There may be a couple of items we might use, old boy, but as it stands there's not a bloody hope – commercially, I mean, as is.'

'I see.' How could Lindsay tell from so few pages? Edward drew a deep breath. 'Matter of fact I've progressed a lot since then – the new idea I thought we'd talk about last Monday at your place.'

'Oh? Let's hear it.'

'Not on the phone,' Edward said.

'Christ, old boy, it's not state bloody secrets – I'm off

to Hayman Sunday, remember?'

Edward felt he had every justification for secrecy. 'It'll keep, I'll work on it while you're away.'

Lindsay laughed. 'You aiming to cut me out, old boy?'

Edward wasn't in a joking mood. 'I just feel I'm on to a good idea.'

Lindsay mocked in a voice of amusing menace, 'You won't get away with it, Piper.'

Edward knew Lindsay was kidding, but knew also that Lindsay was laughing *at* him, at his amateur status. On top of that was his suspicion that Lindsay's flippancy masked the intention to filch. Where were Lindsay's own ideas? Lovers in nude scenes? It was insulting. Edward could clam up too. Lindsay was sharp as a tack, wasn't he? Thought Edward the innocent might come up with something usable.

'Have a nice time at Hayman Island,' he said.

Lindsay laughed. 'Nice is hardly the apt bloody word, old boy. I'll be in there swinging, keeping the jolly old end up, need the breather to tackle number three.'

'You finished the second play?'

'Like a bloody dream. Well, old boy, I'll give you a ring when I get back, and good luck with the new idea.'

Well, that was that. Now it was up to him, Edward felt. Good luck with the new idea – the more he thought about it the more contemptuous it sounded in his ears.

Next morning he fixed the curtains. It was the sort of job he enjoyed, getting the rod up evenly on its supports, the acorns precisely equidistant from each wall. The rain was keeping on.

Sibyl called, 'You doing the shopping, sugar?'

'No.'

'Don't blame you, I ought to be *sacked*. Shan't be longer than twenty-four hours.'

Good-natured Sibyl. Getting away with what she could but generous when she failed. It made him think of the parents. He dreaded their popping in as was their wont before Christmas. The thought of it put him on edge with anxiety. Sibyl would start wheedling again about spending Christmas in the holiday house. He saw the week-end as a pile-up of pressures: Daddy's condescension, Mummy's cosy threats, Sibyl's soft naggings and arm-twistings, rain, mud and a prawny humidity, no doubt a stream of Sibyl's droppers-in. He was under enough pressure with Lindsay's thing and with wanting to wipe the superior smile from Lindsay's face.

So that when the day slid by in peace and quiet Edward felt cheated by a justified tension turning out to be unwarranted. Cheated, too, by Sibyl's creative afternoon while he did nothing, starting at sounds, waiting with stretched nerves for every car to stop.

In the evening, after doing the day's dishes, he pottered on in the kitchen, scrubbing at Sibyl's grime. It helped subdue the suffocated feeling he had. Two edgy cats kept an eye on him. Sibyl was watching television, he could hear dialogue, pauses, explosions and bursts of music. Slabs of life tailored into time-slots. It struck him as odd he'd never seen anything of Lindsay's. Had it been a subconscious avoidance of the envy he tried to suppress? Edward found it impossible to imagine Lindsay writing warm human dialogue in warm human situations. Smarty-pants Lindsay. Edward shoved a cat aside with his foot just as Sibyl came in cuddling the third.

'*Darling*, that's not like you.'

'Sorry. It wasn't a kick.'

Sibyl stooped down and let go the cat she held so she could cuddle the one with the injured vanity. 'Poor little pussy, did the nasty man kickems?'

Edward tightened his lips. When it came to the gratification of needs and wants, the cats had it all over him. He felt the smothering again. Why couldn't she stay with the television? He'd like his own kitchen, his very own, silent.

'Did Daddy say he'd come to Mummy's bedroom to-night?' Sibyl asked the cat in a low voice Edward was meant to hear. The cat arched in ecstasy under her hands. Sibyl looked up with a smile. 'Pussy says yes.'

Edward gave her an unwilling smile. 'All right, darling.'

She was in bed waiting when he got there, eager to love him, her eyes open. Eager for him to love her. He knew his reluctance would vanish under her caresses; like the cat he'd submit to ecstasy. As always she'd sweetened her breath. They began with a touching of lips. But all that happened to Edward was a feeling of irritability with the love play. The tricks of arousal fell flat, the whole thing too much of an effort. He couldn't shut out the taste of dead cigarettes. Nothing was happening. Nothing was going to. There was a lot on his mind preventing sexual excitement. It was the first time he'd felt like this in bed with Sibyl. He felt he couldn't breathe. The stifling had become a physical thing.

'It's all right, darling,' Sibyl said softly. Then slowly and dreamily she tried again with kisses and touches, stroking him with her strong fingers. The hands creatively moulding her clay. Edward brushed them away and sat up suddenly. Sibyl stroked his back.

'All right, sugar, let's forget it. Don't go yet, I'm lonely in here all alone.'

Edward lay down again on his back and cradled Sibyl's head against his arm. Oddly he felt released, as though it had happened after all. He guessed his energy was being redirected into shaping his idea.

'We're having the party on the twelfth now, darling, not the fifth because it conflicts with the Spensers'. Okay?'

Edward squeezed her arm. Start with a plant, or any one organic thing; i.e. an aspect of ecology. Lindsay would say it was his old slant. Lindsay would say he'd done bloody nothing. But Edward's mind had gone full circle to come back to its simplicity. Didn't that prove it stood the test? Didn't that make it cogent?

'You're not listening.'

'Mmm?'

'I said I don't know how you can *bear* to not want to see my potting progress. There's quite a few bits stored away ready in the dining-room.'

'I don't know why you call it the dining-room.'

'That's changing the subject, sugar.'

Lindsay would still have a fictional family. Edward saw himself and Sibyl and young Edward, down to earth, earth-bound like all humanity, demonstrating total ecology via one simple aspect. A complicated message easy for every-one to grasp, to be fired with.

'How're you making out with Lindsay, darling?'

Edward jerked his arm away and got out of bed.

'It *is* Lindsay, isn't it?'

Edward moved to the door.

'Ever since this silly film cropped up you've been so *different*.'

'That's nonsense,' Edward said quietly. He saw she was sitting up, a forlorn shape with the rain's steady drizzle outside.

'That room, all the furniture you've bought, we're like *strangers*, I can't seem to get *near* you, always a frown, and then tonight, that's part of it – why don't you give it up, darling? You *know* you'll never get anywhere.'

Edward went out and shut the door. Locked in his room he dismissed Sibyl's words. Sibyl, after all, liked things as they were, herself the creative one, comfortably deprecating her own talent so Edward didn't feel bad about it.

Stretched on his divan, listening to the rain, his mind wandered off on a vision of a world that was whole, where grubby little things that were ninety-five per cent of real life simply didn't exist.

CHAPTER XI

Sibyl was out all day Sunday. Edward felt in some way
cheated again. And lonely. He looked at his herbs but
there seemed no point with the parsley dead, the new
rosemary already sickly and the mint too lusty by half.
A surfeit of water, perhaps, but that was out of his hands.
The rain had stopped but not the clouds, or the ominous
feeling of more on the way. He filled in the day with housework. Almost he tore down the bead curtain but a surge of
tenderness for Sibyl stopped him. He even stroked the
cats. The parents held off. A safe and spiritless week-end.

CHAPTER XII

Lindsay whooping it up on Hayman Island. The thought
angered Edward and made the days drag. Did Lindsay
care at all about the film? Only, Edward guessed, if a
saleable idea (Edward's) dropped into his lap. Lindsay
didn't waste time on long shots; there was always demand
for his work. It was around two months now since Lindsay
had asked for his help – well, anyway, his views, which
came to the same thing. It seemed to Edward too long a
time to be still fooling around on the hows and whats.

At home there was no solace. Sibyl's party that wasn't
till Friday week seemed already begun in a flap of preparations, and on Wednesday evening when he got in
the uranium committee had the living-room for their
final argument of the year. Edward got a gin and tonic
in the kitchen and took it upstairs. In his room he was able
to shut out their voices. He stood at the window with his

drink. The housing development was less bleak screened by the weave of his curtains. He couldn't shut out his anger.

He went downstairs for a refill. In the hall he met Wally Jones coming from the kitchen with a big dish of savouries. Wally gave him a sheepish smile and sidled into the living-room. Wally had pimples; his father owned the hardware store.

Sibyl was in the kitchen. '*Darling,* I didn't know you were *home,* we're almost done so dinner won't be long.' She picked up two more platters. '*I* know, sugar, come and join in, it's *uranium* – you know, *ecology.*' She gave him a teasing sort of challenging grin Edward didn't like.

'Too tired. You carry on, darling, there's no hurry.'

Sibyl pouted a kiss at him and left with the food. Leave it in the earth: not likely, Edward thought.

He got his drink and went back to his room. He thought of the meeting only in terms of slimy scraps caught in the fringes of rugs, sat upon on cushions, lost in the crevices of armchairs. He should rise above all that, as Sibyl did with her boundless optimism. Boundless and very stupid with present uranium policies. The Spensers weren't on this committee. Perhaps they had uranium shares. That made them sensible, didn't it? Wasn't the film just as stupidly optimistic as Sibyl's activities? Wasn't he stupidly optimistic about Lindsay's intentions, about Lindsay's ethics?

The only relief all week was in his room. The only grab at peace. Sibyl was off in another world, a place he had no interest in. The film in his head took new paths, grew with embellishments of character and sub-plot. He, the hero, was more than a brilliant ecologist, he was also a writer of genius. There was an enemy of earth who had the build of Lindsay, with Lindsay's face, Lindsay's side-ways moronic smile. The film that was just a dream was all his reality in those long waiting days and nights, and he clung to it. Apart from his earlier random notes he had nothing on paper. With the means at hand he dried up; seated at his desk in the environment he'd been at such pains to contrive resentment started, turning again into anger. Anger at anything: at himself, the weather; at Sibyl's silly laughing cheerfulness; but most of all at Lindsay.

He went with Sibyl on Friday to the Spensers' party, held a glass all night, smiled and listened, listened and smiled, drove home around four with Sibyl's head on his shoulder, and remembered nothing of it but a blank in time.

Then at last it was Saturday with Lindsay due back tomorrow. And so what? Would he be in touch? He'd said so, for what it was worth. While Edward did the week-end shopping he tried to capture his idea, crystal clear as it should be, but anger flared obscuring it. He stared at the first cherries. When it came to the point the idea would come pat, he'd tell it to Lindsay in a few words. If Lindsay phoned as he'd said he would.

Lindsay did. Around ten on Monday morning. He sounded on the ball. He sounded happy and excited.

'Great news, old boy, bloody marvellous. Wanna hear?'

'Of course.' Excitement rose.

'How's about my place tomorrow night? Can do?'

Edward's hesitation was momentary. 'Yes, of course.'

'No Diana, promise.' Lindsay laughed. 'No foreign bodies whatever.'

Edward laughed too. 'Have a good time at Hayman?'

'Christ, yes, cut a bloody swathe. Brought you a giftie. Sixish tomorrow then?'

'Fine.'

Edward got through the day somehow. It could be only one thing: Lindsay had backing for the film. That was the only exciting news he'd want to tell Edward about. Perhaps someone he'd met at Hayman Island. More likely word received back in town. Who cared about the way of it? Edward wished it were tonight they were meeting. Lindsay must have something on tonight, maybe a celebration. Edward thought he should be in on the celebration. Then he thought no, Lindsay's kind of celebration wasn't his. Great news, Lindsay had said. Edward was so happy he even forgave the weather.

And the parents who were there when he got home. Edward hugged Mummy and kissed her cheek, then shook Daddy's hand and clapped him on the back. Sibyl stood watching with a pleased little wary smile, so for good measure, and because he wanted to terribly, Edward hugged her too.

'*Gosh,* darling, you come into a *fortune* or something?'

Edward grinned and hugged her again. 'Goodwill season, just starting a mite early.'

Daddy finished the whisky he had. 'Well, come on, better get going if we're going,' he said in his cheery bossy voice.

Sibyl said in a quick nervous way, 'They're taking us out to dinner, darling, okay? Daddy's booked for seven, you can have a drink there.'

'Fine, everything's fine and dandy.' He could even forgo a shower, even tolerate Daddy's presumptions and Mummy's pink excited nose. Only the cats looked hard-done-by.

Edward took his own car because the parents were driving straight on down the coast after dinner. Sibyl went in the parents' car.

Their table was as jolly as any in the restaurant. Sibyl looked happy, now and again giving Edward private little smiles. Once she squeezed his thigh under the table and Edward responded with a throb of passion. Daddy said the river was swollen with the rains. Mummy said she was up to her ears in the church bazaar. Daddy said farmers were worried by the weather bureau's warnings. Mummy said she was making a patchwork quilt for their holiday cottage.

'You're coming down, of course,' Daddy stated.

Sibyl looked hesitant. 'We are, aren't we, sugar?'

Edward couldn't stop smiling. 'Better not count on me, looks as if a project I'm working on'll keep my nose to the grindstone all over Christmas and New Year.' He couldn't stop the smile. This was happiness.

'Got to take time off, son. All work and no play,' Daddy said, making Edward a dull boy with more success than if he'd actually said it. 'What's the project?' he added as an afterthought.

'Besides,' Mummy said, 'there's Sibyl to think of,' and pressed Edward's other thigh in a sort of morse containing threat.

'There's everyone to think of,' Edward said smiling and shifting a bit.

'Of *course*,' Sibyl put in quickly.

'Glad you agree,' Daddy said, taking it as settled.

The rest of the meal passed in the same jolly fashion. Mummy got on to the quilt again and Daddy on to the flood danger. Mummy's nose was red. As they waved the parents off Edward sighed, feeling the strain he hadn't felt in their presence.

They made love that night. Afterwards Sibyl said, 'You've had good news from Lindsay, haven't you, darling?'

'The best, darling.' He didn't say he'd be late home tomorrow. Sibyl set no store by trivial courtesies. He began to kiss her again and the throb returned. He stayed all night with Sibyl in her bed.

On Tuesday when Lindsay opened his door he said, 'Christ, old boy, you're prompt.'

Edward smiled. The hour he'd filled in at the office had been an eternity. 'You look very well.' Lindsay had a pinkish sort of tan which was no adornment.

'It's all the depravity.' Lindsay grinned. 'Come on in, old boy.'

Lindsay got them drinks then led the way into his workroom. It gave their meeting a businesslike start that pleased Edward. Lindsay looked businesslike too, seated in his chair behind the desk; the raffishness was something he couldn't help. Edward sat facing him in a comfortable straight-backed chair with an orange vinyl seat.

'Oh, nearly forgot.' Lindsay picked up a tissue-wrapped package on the desk and tossed it at Edward. 'What I brought you from Hayman.'

Edward's pleasure vanished when he opened it up. What Lindsay called a giftie was a dreadful bright blue tie with a vulgar pink nude girl on it. 'Thanks very much,' he said.

'Well, old boy, how's it shaping? What progress?'

Edward hesitated, then said, 'Have you made any?'

Lindsay laughed. 'Have *I* made any! – Christ, old boy, wait'll you hear, and all the bloody time having it off on Hayman.'

It seemed to Edward that he must speak first, that that was as it should be in the circumstances: Lindsay the professional, Edward his protégé. 'Yes, I've made progress, excellent progress, I think. I've come, so to speak, full circle.'

'Blow me down,' Lindsay said, 'what kind of full circle would that be?'

Edward leaned forward to impress. 'I've thought the whole subject through and through from every angle and it just won't work, visually or sequentially, unless we start as I suggested in the first place – with a single organic growth.'

Lindsay waited. Edward didn't like the half-smile through his smoke.

'We can keep the family you suggested,' Edward went

on, feeling on top of his subject. 'I know you were joking about nude lovers, but naturally there've got to be people and a well-knit family group identifies with the aim – you see what I mean? – everything well-knit, a well-knit ecology.'

'Seems a lot of bloody knitting. Anything on paper?'

'I think first I'd like to know what you think about it.'

Lindsay stubbed out his cigarette. The ashtray was a huge square of thick green glass. He leaned back in his chair and got out a fresh cigarette, picked up the lighter and lit it. He didn't look at Edward, while Edward followed every move and tried to gauge Lindsay's expression. At last Lindsay's eyes met his.

'Look, old boy, we'll have to shelve it a while, maybe even scrap the whole idea.'

Edward was stunned, speechless. Lindsay wasn't smiling.

'Something's come up, the best, old boy. There may be a chance to get back to this later but I wouldn't count on it, not the rate you're going.'

Edward's head seemed to swell. One thought was clear: he was not going to have identity and purpose snatched from him, not in this cavalier way, not in any way. He couldn't speak.

Lindsay took a swig and a puff, a superior smile on his degenerate face. 'I've been commissioned to write the script for the film of Greenacre's book – you know, old boy, Wayne Greenacre, wrote *All the Pub's Men* and landed a runaway local bestseller. Read it?'

Edward shook his head.

'Sends up Aussie mateship, bloody bang-on filmwise.' His eyes were laughing at Edward. 'Well, old boy, how's about the old congrats?'

Edward said, 'It should be right up your alley.' He was angry, too angry to choose words, so angry he scarcely knew what he said. And with a horrible emptiness.

Lindsay made a face. 'Bit bloody grudging, old boy,

but thanks all the same.' He seemed unaware of what he was doing to Edward. The wreckage. He thought Edward should exult with him. 'Be travelling around a lot, locations and stuff, outback and city pubs, bloody goodoh.' Twisting the knife in the death wound. 'Well now,' he leaned back puffing lazily, 'we might as well call a halt on the other thing, no point now, you wouldn't stand a chance on your own.'

The truth came in a flash to Edward. Lindsay was lying. Lindsay had Edward's nutshell idea and meant to ditch him. Edward didn't believe the commission story. Lindsay's plan was to pinch Edward's idea, ransack Edward's brains. Lindsay was a turd.

Edward said in a low controlled voice, 'It's as much mine now as yours, more.'

Lindsay stared, then laughed. 'Christ, old boy, you don't think I really needed bloody help from *you*?'

'You've wormed out all my ideas.'

'You've got to be bloody joking.' Lindsay got up, laughing. His ash missed the ashtray. 'For Chris'sake grow up, old boy, what ideas? You lack the knack. Put it down as a bit of fun. No skin off anyone's nose. The so-called partnership's over.'

Edward stared at Lindsay. 'And my contribution – you're just going to walk off with it?'

'Walk off with what?' Lindsay eyed him. 'You're way off beam, old boy. If you mean this – ' he pulled out a drawer of his desk and ratted through it, then pulled out the few sheets of foolscap – 'take it by all means.' He dropped the pages in front of Edward.

Edward felt sick. He couldn't believe it. His friend Lindsay. Lindsay who'd opened the door and was now blocking the doorway. He had to believe it. He picked up the pages and folded them in half. 'I've got rights in the work.'

'What work? Look, feller, you're beginning to bore

me.' Lindsay's smile was gone. 'You're an envious little toad, Piper, that's all there bloody is to it.'

Little! Lindsay calling him little! Edward went on folding the pages until they formed a tight wad. 'You asked for my help,' he said in a dead voice.

'Christ, a bit of a lark. I don't say it mightn't have come to something given certain things. Could have been in the bloody bag by now.'

'If *you'd* had any ideas.'

'If your bloody bitch of a wife had come good – you've got a dead weight there, old boy.'

There was no point. Lindsay had a coarseness for everything. Edward groped for a final word, something dignified, then he'd go. 'You owe me thirty dollars,' he said.

'Christ, take it, feller.' Lindsay got out his wallet and flung three tens at Edward. 'Now you can bloody go. I made a mistake, thought you'd be glad at my good fortune – Christ! As for the bloody ecology thing, say it was just a tease – believe you me, I've been sick a long time of your hangdog bloody envy. This other thing's all set up.'

'I don't believe you.' Edward was motionless, his hand gripped on the wad of paper.

'Check up, then.' Lindsay came out with a string of names, dates, sums of money. 'You get on to them, old boy, don't take my word for it. I'm a bloody professional, mate. You don't pull it out of a hat like a bloody rabbit. You've got to have what it takes and you haven't got it, old boy, not the faintest bloody spark of – '

While Lindsay was talking Edward stood up. He didn't know he was standing up, all he knew was Lindsay's face in front of him, little Lindsay's face, looking up with the bloodshot eyes, the smile gone, looking scared. Then Lindsay was on the floor and there was blood on his forehead. He lay still. He looked unconscious. Edward staggered round Lindsay's desk and lowered himself slowly into Lindsay's chair. What he'd done stunned him. He hadn't meant to. He wasn't a violent man. Yet he'd wanted something somehow to smite Lindsay so in a way had meant it. Yet he hadn't meant it. His right hand ached. He stared at the square green ashtray it was holding. Ash and stubs were spilled on the desk and floor. He heard sounds. Traffic, music. He went to the bathroom with the ashtray and washed it, holding it under running hot water, drying it with paper towels. He took it back to the workroom and put it on the desk. He picked up the thirty dollars. He went back for more paper towels, water-dampened, and cleaned up the ash and stubs. Then he picked up the wad of paper which had fallen to the floor and stuffed it in his pocket. The tie and its tissue wrapping went into his other pocket. The restoration of order pleased him.

Only then he remembered Lindsay. Wasn't it time Lindsay was coming round? He went down on his haunches. Lindsay looked dead. He couldn't be. Edward didn't remember the blow but was sure it hadn't had force enough for that. Just a spot of blood. Lindsay's left arm lay neatly beside him, the right was somehow across his chin as though he'd been warding off something. Edward felt for Lindsay's pulse. There was none. None in his neck. His heart had stopped. He'd had a heart attack.

Edward got up. His legs were trembling so he could hardly stand. He went for more paper towels, moving like someone just out of bed after a long illness. He took his glass to the kitchen. There was a whole stack of glasses and stuff needed washing. Just like Sibyl. Edward tipped out the drink, wiped the outside of the glass and put it among the others. He put all the paper towels he'd used in Lindsay's kitchen bin, poking them down among the other refuse. The sink had a disposal unit but Edward dreaded the noise it would make. Back in the workroom he got out his handkerchief and wiped everything he might have touched; there wasn't much: the chair, the desk, Lindsay's chair, perhaps the doors. He left Lindsay's glass where it was, a man given to drinking. Then he went, checking first that the other tenants on Lindsay's floor weren't about. There were only two units to a floor. His legs felt better. He left Lindsay's front door open. Anyone could get in. Anyone could have got in. Some enemy of Lindsay's. He'd left no evidence. He thought with a shock: I'm thinking like a murderer. It was absurd. Lindsay couldn't be dead. He couldn't believe Lindsay was dead. He'd known Lindsay a long time. Lindsay was so alive. His car was parked in the next street at a meter. Lindsay's place said Residents' Cars Only. His car wouldn't be remembered. There, he was doing it again. Edward smiled at himself.

CHAPTER XIII

'Did you bring up the flagons, sugar?'

'Yes, darling.'

Hauling two flagons of cheap red from the pottery was just one of several jobs Edward had done at Sibyl's behest before the guests should arrive. It was his first visit to the pottery in months and he'd expected to find it stuffed with exhibition gems. But there was just the old mucky jumble and the usual few pedestrian bits on the shelves. He remembered then she was storing her treasures in the dining-room.

He'd come home to the impression of a fun-fair and Sibyl animated in a cyclamen pants suit outside an open, waiting house. She'd run to meet him.

'Like it, sugar?'

She'd got an odd-job man with a lawn mower and a lot of coloured lights. The lights outlined the pottery and the back porch, they were strung across the wasteland, stuck in the straggly old gum trees and even arranged to light up the castor oil, with sinister effect. Over all was an air of dismal gaiety, but Edward, unlike the cats, hid his depression.

'Lovely, darling.'

Now Sibyl had gone upstairs for last-minute touches and Edward waited in the primped-up living-room where every tassel and fringe looked freshly inimical. The rainbow lights were here, too, fighting the usual reds and oranges.

He felt at a loss without Lindsay. Nothing had meaning. Even his room: it had been built around Lindsay. There was no point to it now. He felt adrift. He seemed to remember a headlong sensation of loss, then this drained emptiness.

That night when he got home there'd been three ten dollar notes in his jacket pocket. Lindsay must have paid him back, that was decent of Lindsay. Then he remembered asking Lindsay and felt ashamed. He couldn't believe he'd been so ignoble. Lindsay was the ignoble one. In a burst of choked sentiment he'd hung the hideous tie with his own ties. The wad of paper, his precious foolscap pages, he'd flung from his window into the wasteland.

It had been in the paper Wednesday morning, shocking in its confirmation. He'd hidden it from Sibyl. 'Brilliant Playwright Found Dead.' Edward thought bitterly the brilliance was death's doing. It went on to say that Lindsay Reid, well-known scriptwriter, had just been commissioned to write the screenplay for Wayne Greenacre's – so it was true. He couldn't read to the end. His strong hands twisted the newspaper into a rope. Edward might have been brilliant too with Lindsay's help, if Lindsay had been sincere, just the least bit sincere about anything at all. That same night near the end of dinner Sibyl said, 'What on earth's *up,* Eddie, you've eaten absolutely *nothing.*' Edward said the humidity.

Then yesterday a detective named Lumley called at the office mid-morning to see Edward. A discreet, pleasant man

with a grey felt hat. Edward liked him at once. Just a
formality, Lumley said. There might be someone among
Mr Reid's friends who could throw some light on the
mystery. Edward said he was merely Mr Reid's tax accountant. Lumley was tall and thin, dark and pale, and wore
unostentatious glasses with thin tortoiseshell rims and brown
eyes. Edward thought he looked ill, at any rate unhealthy.
His voice was quiet and had a gentleness. He sat in the
chair Lindsay threw his briefcase in. Had Mr Piper seen
Mr Reid recently? Not since the week before last. Edward
hadn't liked telling the lie. He could imagine Lumley
becoming his friend. He could talk with Lumley. Lumley
had a sober, responsible face. Nothing pushy about him.
If he could explain to Lumley mightn't Lumley understand? In other circumstances they'd have found a lot
in common, Edward felt sure. When Lumley smiled he
looked less ill but a lot sadder. He'd be in his forties,
Edward thought. He'd gone away satisfied, thanking
Edward. Edward was sorry he wouldn't see Lumley again.

The same night when he got home – only last night? –
Sibyl pounced with the news.

'*Lindsay*'s dead.'

A wave of nausea made him groggy.

'Didn't you *know*?'

He shook his head. He slumped at the kitchen table.

'Diana rang, it happened on Tuesday some time, the
neighbour found his door open, *foul play*, he'd been *struck*
with something – Eddie, you're not *listening*.'

'I am, it's – the shock.'

'Who on earth would kill *Lindsay*?'

'People didn't like him – you, for instance.'

'*Eddie*!'

Edward stood up.

'Diana thinks a burglar probably panicked.' Edward
escaped but Sibyl followed him part way upstairs. 'What
about Lindsay's good news you had?'

'Over the phone.'

Locked in his room he'd felt dead. His room felt dead. Mostly it was long blank hours without beginning or end. The party was suddenly in full swing. Instant people seeping everywhere. In the dining-room, which Sibyl could clear miraculously if she chose to, even of her little exhibition treasures. Upstairs, on the stairs, in the hall, on the never-used front verandah beneath Edward's room, all over the rough, stubby, mown grass, looking ill in the reds, greens and blues of Sibyl's lights. Already a disorganized mess with none of the martial order the Spensers' affairs had. Sibyl's party was Sibyl projected, slapdashery on a grand scale.

Was this his fourth or fifth gin and tonic? It was pleasant, this woozy feeling. It kept thoughts at bay. Edward took a back seat in the crowd round the barbecue, which served as an outdoor bar and where Colin Jones and Wally Jones (unrelated) were dispensing rum-and-cokes and the cheap red. Sibyl had hired a bunch of hard identical chairs. There seemed to be stars. It hadn't rained for days.

Had he struck Lindsay? It was just so unlikely. He simply wasn't that sort of person. He never even raised his voice in anger, Sibyl was always marvelling at that. He remembered feeling more disgusted than angry. He'd felt no anger when Lindsay abused Sibyl. Then Edward's heart began to pound as he heard Lindsay's voice saying those shattering things, saying he was bored, sick of Edward's envy; calling Edward a little toad and finally jeering at Edward's aspirations.

'Are you all right, Edward?'

He stared at Nance Clifford who was looking at him with concern. Edward relaxed the grip he had on his glass. 'Fine, just the noise.' Then he started to laugh.

'What is it?'

'Nothing.' Nance wouldn't see how funny the coloured

lights were, like a circus. How sickly she looked, they all looked, even the moths and beetles flying in the multi-glare that defeated Sibyl's purpose.

'I'd better find Jeff.' Nance got up, looking a bit put out.

Edward watched her go. Comfortable, plump, uncomplicated Nance. Lucky Jeff. His eyes met Diana's fixed on him from under her hair across the barbecue, between bodies. It gave him a shock. Sibyl changing her party date had made it possible for Diana to come. Natural enough that she should, an old friend. All the same he got up and went inside the house. On the way he saw a man and two women, strangers, smiling at his herbs.

In the living-room a bunch of people were shouting and laughing at once, Sibyl among them. Edward hoped to remain unnoticed. There was more chance of being passed over if he stayed put like a cushion or lampshade. When had they ever noticed him except as Sibyl's husband? Then all at once Diana was there too. Her eyes flicked over him.

He heard Sibyl. 'It's *dreadful* about Lindsay, have they found out anything yet?'

Edward moved to the sideboard. Its litter sickened him. He could feel Diana's eyes on his back. He heard bits of things.

'What luck the rain holding off after –'

'You mean *murdered*?'

'Just like Julie's, sort of knife pleats down the –'

'June I think, it's amazing how she does it what with all the –'

'Not *this* year, darling, we're off down the coast, that's if I can twist Eddie's arm.'

'The detective thinks –'

Parties were always the same: shouting, headaches and a lot of cleaning and washing-up for him to do afterwards. They seemed to have forgotten him. Sibyl, Diana, Max and Julie Spenser, Sibyl's new black friend Brian Something, met at a meeting, six or seven other people, strangers he'd met perhaps at some time.

'You should see his den.' Sibyl's laughing voice.

Edward turned, met all their eyes. 'Without a single flounce,' he said.

Julie's wry smile took his meaning.

'He's spent a *fortune* on it,' Sibyl laughed, 'just imagine, in *these* times, only the very best imported for Eddie. While I slave away potting to *pay* for it all.'

Edward forced a smile. 'She pots to fill in her time.'

Everyone laughed at the unlikely notion that Sibyl had time to fill. Sibyl too. But not Diana, whose eyes on him were sombre.

Edward felt wretchedly at bay. He could strangle Sibyl. 'The truth is it's a dodge to occupy the liberated woman who insisted on marriage.'

There was a silence. Couldn't they take a joke? He'd meant it as a joke, hadn't he? Sibyl showed her hurt and bewilderment. Someone attempted a laugh. It was himself.

'Having a little hobby keeps her out of mischief,' he said. But it was only silence again as Edward walked from the room.

There was a bustle in the kitchen where Nance and Jeff were organizing the catered food and a string of jolly helpers. Edward went out to the garden again. He wished he could go to his room. But his room was anathema now. He saw Helen Jones sitting alone removed from the noisy group round the barbecue. Edward went over to her. She had a dreamy inward smile. She was Colin's wife and a baby was on the way. Colin was a carpenter and Helen worked in a chemist's shop. It was Helen who'd found the bead curtains they all had. But Edward didn't blame Helen for the thing that daily infuriated him.

He dropped on the prickly stubs of coarse grass. 'This is not much in your line, is it?'

Helen smiled down at him. 'Not these days, not any time, really. Watch out you don't get piles.'

Edward laughed. 'Won't have a chance to be here long enough.'

'Isn't Sibyl wonderful?'

'Marvellous.'

'All she does. Just two organizations I'm run off my feet, and even then I'm no leading light. But Sibyl copes with everything, and then her lovely ceramics.'

'Yes.'

'You must be terribly proud of her, Edward.'

'I am.'

'Plus meals and marketing, then all the housework on top.'

'And three cats,' Edward said.

Forks, napkins and plates of stuff were shoved into their hands. Edward put his on the grass beside him. 'Can you manage all right?' he asked.

'Yes thanks. And Edward?'

'Yes?'

'I think you're wonderful too, I think you're a darling.'

'Thank you.'

'You're so sort of, oh – so restful. And sober. I wish – ' she stopped.

Edward knew she was thinking of Colin. The comparison was hard to avoid with Colin right in front of their eyes staggering as he pulled a giggling girl about.

'Things work themselves out,' Edward said.

They sat in a comfortable silence. Edward supposed he should make some effort at chat. Ask about the baby. He hated shouted conversation. The noise was deafening. Lucky for neighbours they weren't cheek by jowl. Helen seemed content, eating whatever it was and absorbed again by the miracle inside her.

At last he stood up. His muscles felt stiff. He'd had no exercise lately. He smiled at her. 'If I don't go and do

my bit that superwoman'll cut my ears off. You okay?
Want anything?'

'No, thanks. You've eaten nothing.'

'Not hungry.' He picked up the things.

She smiled. 'All right, better go and do your duty.'

A few people seemed on the point of drifting off.
Edward sighed. His duty. What was his duty? Wasn't
it to himself? Half-eaten food about everywhere. It was
the same inside, Sibyl in the hall with her overlong
farewells, plates with remains of food stuck on window
sills, on the stairs, on chairs. Edward stood a bit behind
Sibyl, smiling, silent, on edge.

It seemed for ever. At last when only the Cliffords and
Diana were left Edward murmured good night and escaped
upstairs. He heard Nance's voice: 'Edward's losing weight.'

He left the door of his room open because the stifling
was in here too. He looked through his curtains at the
night. High up was the new thin moon. The sky looked
airy, relieved. Shouldn't he feel the same with Lindsay
gone? It seemed unfair. Hadn't Lindsay been a torment
of Edward's own making? In trying to measure up he'd
conjured the unbearable pressure Lindsay exerted. Now the
weight was gone, wasn't it? And wasn't the weather a
symbol of that?

He heard the last repetitious goodbye shouts. He felt
caught, suffocating.

Sibyl's quick feet on the stairs. 'Enjoy the party, sugar?'

Edward turned smiling from the window but made no
reply. Adapt, he told himself. He knew it was now or
never.

'You got a bit nasty about my pots, darling. After all,
I was potting before I even *met* you.' Her smile teased in
a friendly way.

'And you got nasty about my room.' His voice was mild
as always.

'*Gosh*, can't you take a *joke*? Brian was very surprised

at what you said.'

He imagined their conversation. Sibyl discussing him with strangers: it was intolerable. 'Is he also surprised by your disgusting squalor?'

Sibyl looked miserable then. He thought she might go, wanted her to go. But Sibyl liked things thrashed out and resolved. 'I'm sorry, darling, I really will try. You too.'

'Me too what?'

'Well – try not to be quite so *critical*, perhaps.'

'I feel critical.'

'Why suddenly now?'

'It's not suddenly now. It's years of it. '

'We're having a row, aren't we? You've been itching for one all evening.'

Edward was silent.

Sibyl looked frustrated. 'If you'd only get wild and *throw* something.'

'You want me to?'

'Oh, *I* don't know – no, of *course* not.' She went to the window and twitched the curtain aside, then let it drop. 'I *know* you're in a rage, I *always* know, so why don't you ever shout like other people?'

'Would it help?'

Her sigh was overdue. 'I suppose not, sugar, it just seems *unnatural.*'

'Isn't sugar?'

'Yes, I suppose –' she looked close to tears. 'It's only an endearment.'

Edward leaned his rump against the desk and crossed his feet. A Lindsay nonchalance. The twisted smile he felt on his face was Lindsay's smile. He'd just thought of something Lindsay would like: insert Brian into the script. Sibyl, the perfect helpmeet, falls in love with Brian, better than nude scenes, or incorporate nude scenes, black body and white, white with carroty hair, Lindsay would marvel at his brainwave, Sibyl's name was Rachel, Lindsay would marvel and admire, bloody bang-on.

'You're not even listening,' Sibyl said.

He looked at her.

'I said I'll try to remember about sugar and I'll try with the muddle too, darling, I really will *try,* I mean it – lots of New Year resolutions.'

'I see.'

'You don't sound impressed.'

'We've seen them collapse so often, haven't we? As the days go trundling by.'

'I know, Eddie, but do be fair, you know how busy I am. I thought you understood. I think you ought to encourage me.' Then in a low voice she added, 'Even *emulate.*'

Edward smiled.

The smile riled Sibyl. 'You only blame me to excuse yourself. *You're* what's collapsing, Eddie.'

'The perfect helpmeet.' If only she'd go. He went to the window. He'd like to fly away beyond the moon.

Sibyl burst out, 'What d'you expect, *grovelling*?'

Edward sighed. He turned to face her. 'Now we see your other side,' he said in his calm voice.

'We've all got another side and they're all unbearable.'

'So is Eddie unbearable.'

Sibyl turned to his bookshelves and pretended to look at his books. Then to his desk, flipping over one of Lindsay's scripts. Trying to stop the tears, Edward thought. But what she said almost caught him off guard. 'You were late home the night Lindsay was killed. Where were you?'

It came easily, after all. 'In the office. Very accommodating of *you* to be home for once.'

But Sibyl rejected the bait. 'Diana says they're sure it was someone who knew Lindsay well.'

'They'd better start with Diana, then, hadn't they?'

Sibyl frowned.

'You sure you've got time for detecting on top of potting?'

'We had a long talk.'

'I can imagine.' He hated the thing she was wearing.

'I don't know what's the matter with you tonight,' Sibyl said. 'Gosh, what an end to a party, we're supposed to feel relaxed and *happy*.' She sighed and moved to the door.

Make Brian a potter. A black potter would be arresting. Lindsay's thing needed a shot in the arm. Arresting, and ecological racewise. And why call it Lindsay's thing? It was his thing: Edward's. Black and white in a grand passion, both potters. The room felt good again.

'You and your daydreams.' Sibyl was in the doorway, a cat winding round her cyclamen pants. 'I said there's masses of clearing-up waiting downstairs.'

Edward thought, your bloody department, old girl.

'It's after two, darling – coming?'

Edward sat at his desk. He liked the feel of his smile. In his head he said, Shut the door as you go, old thing, okay?

Sibyl waited. She had the cat in her arms. 'Darling?'

'Okay.' Edward got up. He followed her downstairs.

On the way Sibyl said, 'You really *are* an angel and I'm sorry. Tomorrow I'm going to wait on you hand and foot and clean the *entire* house from head to toe.'

'Tall order,' Edward said with a smile. Bloody bitch.

It was nearly four before he was done. Sibyl had flaked out around three. Bunch of bloody morons, the lot of them.

It was peaceful in his room. The door locked. The film with its new domestic triangle slant, two whites and a black, unwound excitingly in the dark. It was great.

CHAPTER XIV

Edward had a few moments with Mr Strachan before
Lumley came on Monday morning. It was because Lumley
was coming that Edward had asked to see Mr Strachan.
Edward was nervous. He wanted to tell Mr Strachan,
before Mr Strachan should hear it piecemeal and dis-
torted, that the police wanted Edward's advice in their
inquiries into the death of Lindsay Reid.

'That's a nuisance,' Mr Strachan said, 'for you, I mean,
Mr Piper.'

'Well,' Edward said with a smile, 'I suppose it's up to
me to contribute the little I can.'

'Very good of you. They'll appreciate it. No problems
with his tax, were there?'

'None at all. I expect they just want my estimate of him,
as a man, I mean, as to character.'

'Poor fellow. Well, I suppose they have to do it.
Thank you for letting me know, Mr Piper.' Mr Strachan
gave Edward the warm smile that always looked so
unlikely on his thin pale face on its thin stalk of a neck.

Edward went back to his office. Lumley had telephoned
just after nine and asked whether he might see Edward
at 10.30. He'd asked but it wasn't a question: Lumley was
coming anyway.

For the first time Edward wondered how Lumley had
known about him at all, even to where his office was. Had
he accepted a police visit as inevitable? It shook him a
little to think how he'd acted towards Lumley, as though
reassuring a client. He tried to remember what he'd said
to Lumley. Perhaps he should have asked to be told details
of Lindsay's death, beyond the baldness of the newspaper
story. Yet why should a once-yearly business acquaintance

profess such interest? It seemed safer not to have asked.
If Lumley had set a trap he'd got nowhere. At the same
time he'd seemed too nice a man to resort to tricks. Yet
Lumley had known about him and that was unnerving.

Lumley soon cleared up the question. After a pleasant
good morning and a comment on the miserable weather (a
new low was moving over), after sitting in Lindsay's briefcase chair and putting his hat on the corner of Edward's
desk.

'We're checking through all the names in Mr Reid's
personal telephone index.'

Edward felt relief. He should have thought of that.

'Alphabetically,' Lumley added as if by way of an afterthought.

Edward was nervous again. Hadn't they reached him
too soon?

'Miss Lucas says you were collaborating with Mr Reid
on a story for a film.'

Ah! Edward smiled. 'Miss Lucas must have misunder-
stood, Mr Reid never consulted me about anything other
than taxation matters.' He forgot all about the two old
film scripts of Lindsay's he still had, he forgot everything in his anger against Diana.

'You know Miss Lucas?'

'Hardly at all. She happened to be with my wife at
the theatre the first time we met – that is, my wife and I.'

'That was some years ago?'

'Seven to eight, I'd say, I could work it out exactly.'

'That's all right, Mr Piper, Miss Lucas says the same.'

'Since then I've barely met her.' On impulse he added,
'I don't like her,' and wished it at once unsaid.

'But Mr Reid was very fond of her.'

'Was he?' Edward's interest lapsed suddenly. 'I knew
nothing of Mr Reid's private affairs beyond financial
matters.'

Lumley got out a new-looking notebook. He smiled

at Edward before consulting it. Lumley was simply a nuisance to be got through, like the weather and Sibyl's meetings. Edward felt no concern. He tried to conjure Lindsay but Lindsay was remote, wispy as his unattractive hair. They'd come unstuck, that's all. It happened to people all over. Didn't make you a bloody murderer. Lumley knew this. Lumley meant him no harm. This was his way of seeking co-operation as Edward had sought it from that bloody creep Lindsay. Edward would collaborate with Lumley. Lumley would see through a tramp like Diana. Lumley had a nice face he could trust. Lines he hadn't noticed the first time. Undistinguished, a nice face wearing glasses.

Lumley looked up. 'Miss Goldman finally admitted you were last in the office that night.'

'Which night?'

'The night of Tuesday, December 9th.'

'Would that be – is that the night it happened?'

'Yes, Mr Piper, last Tuesday.'

'I must have been, then,' Edward said in a frank friendly voice. 'I'm often last in the office.'

'What time did you leave?'

Edward laughed. 'We don't punch cards here. My wife might have some idea of the time I got home.' At once he regretted saying that, he didn't want Sibyl brought into this. He didn't want Lumley's innocent little questions drawing out Sibyl's emphatic embroideries. 'My wife's out a lot too, she's on a lot of committees for bettering the world.'

Lumley smiled. 'But she was home that night when you got home?'

Edward shrugged. 'I don't remember.' It was true, all he remembered was the thirty dollars he'd found in one of his pockets. Then he thought that this reply too would set Lumley on to Sibyl. It seemed altogether too careless for a meticulous man like himself not to notice whether his wife was home or not. 'It goes on all the time,' he added with a smile, 'we're both so used to it, often I get my own dinner.'

'I see.' Lumley was writing in his notebook.

Why was Lumley asking all these questions? 'I don't think I quite understand what you're getting at,' Edward said in his pleasant mild voice.

'Just clearing the way, a matter of elimination.' Lumley's smile was comforting.

'Shouldn't you be investigating possible suspects?'

'We are, Mr Piper, don't worry.'

'There must be quite a few, I should think – I mean, from my limited contact with Mr Reid he didn't strike me as a likable man.'

'Ah.' Lumley looked intent. 'Really?'

'Well, a bit cocky, a know-all.' Edward made himself stop. He'd almost said too much then.

But Lumley seemed unperturbed. He just said again, 'I see.' But he made another note.

Edward looked at his watch.

Lumley said, 'It wasn't an ordinary breaking and entering.'

'No?'

'No. It was somebody Mr Reid knew, that much is certain. There's one curious feature.'

'Oh?' A moment's pause. 'May I know?'

'It was someone with the nerve to stop and remove his fingerprints. At the same time he removed a lot of prints that should normally be in evidence. It was also someone with a strong sense of order.'

Edward looked admiring. 'That's really masterly.'

'On the murderer's part?'

Edward smiled. 'On yours.'

'But not on the murderer's part,' Lumley said, 'he was too tidy by half.'

'Or she,' Edward said.

'Or she.'

'I think it's very clever of you to notice things like that.'

'It's just part of the job, Mr Piper, factual evidence plus an understanding of human nature.' He tucked the notebook away in his breast pocket.

'You build up a picture, I suppose.'

'Well, that's a bit fanciful.' Lumley smiled. 'A lot of plodding, really.' He stood up, picked up his hat. 'I'd better let you get on with your own work. Thank you, Mr Piper – no, don't get up.'

When Lumley was at the door Edward said, 'Sounds like a woman, all that tidying up. I've just remembered Mr Reid's women – he boasted a lot, quite tiresomely.'

'Thank you, Mr Piper.' Lumley smiled, nodded and left.

Edward felt dreamy and remote. Things seemed far away; his desk was far away with somebody else seated at it. Had Lumley been here asking questions or was it a new character he'd created in a script development? Mrs Fleming brought in two letters that should have gone on Friday. Not her fault, of course – his for leaving them till the last minute. Nothing was ever Mrs Fleming's fault. Edward signed them.

There's this plodding, unimaginative, clumsy man. His name's Lumley. His clodhopper quality makes him an ideal agent of the enemy organization. Just the sort of smart-Aleck trick the enemy chief Lindsay would think a winner. Lumley's ill sad face is all part of the disguise while he –

'Mr Piper?' Mrs Fleming was back with the two letters and a disconcerted face. 'I'll type them again, Mr Piper.' She held them in front of him so that Edward could see he'd signed 'Lindsay Reid' on both.

Edward managed a smile. 'I'll tell you how that happened, Mrs Fleming – the police have asked me to tell them all I can remember about Mr Reid. He was one of our clients, you know, one of mine.'

'Yes, Mr Piper, I know. I'll do them again. I thought I should tell you.'

'Thanks, Mrs Fleming.' He gave her his nicest smile and watched her go.

Mrs Fleming had a strong sense of order. It wasn't an unusual trait. She could have done the letters again and simply brought them in again for him to sign. An i-dotter and t-crosser, a fusspot in every way, Mrs Fleming to everyone – nobody in the office dared call her Iris. As for Ms, it made her foam at the mouth. Lumley had his work cut out if tidiness were all he had to go on. And there was nothing else, was there?

Miss Goldman was among the load in his lift going down at lunch time. Edward smiled at her but something slid in Miss Goldman's eyes and took them to furtive rest on a man's sleeve buttons. The lift gave Edward a sinking feeling.

After lunch, on the way back, he bought a packet of cigarettes, Lindsay's brand, and a disposable lighter. He'd never smoked before. He thought he might grow in time to like it, when it became a habit. Miss Goldman was back at her reception desk. This time she returned his smile and her eyes went to his cigarette. Observant girl, Miss Goldman.

Mrs Fleming's dreary old letters were on his desk, re-typed. Bloody lot of crap. Edward signed them, then noticed his neat small handwriting. Silly bloody precise habit of a lifetime. He felt a flourishing signature starting and tried it out on his notepad a few times. Not too big, very bold, quick, almost illegible. He liked it.

When Mrs Fleming answered his buzzer around four o'clock she stopped in an uncharacteristic, theatrical way just inside the door. 'You're smoking!'

'Sit down, Mrs Fleming. Four letters. Thanks for these.'

He pushed the two letters on his desk.

Mrs Fleming came to the desk but didn't sit down. 'Lots of people are trying to give it up and you're just starting.'

'I haven't got all day, Mrs Fleming.'

She sat down with her eyes on his ashtray. 'This is your sixth since lunch.'

'I know you can count, Mrs Fleming, ready?' Rage consumed Edward. Silly bloody bitch wasn't his keeper. He stared at the extractions he'd jotted down from the file of Pittwater and Hartog, a building firm. His brain wouldn't function, his concentration was gone. He felt Mrs Fleming's eyes. But they weren't on him, they were on his notepad where he'd tried out his new signature. An ability to read upside down wouldn't be missing from Mrs Fleming's accomplishments.

'Oh, Christ!' Edward said. Something had been niggling.

Mrs Fleming stared at him in horror.

'Christ!' he said again. Then he smiled at her. 'Sorry, old girl, tomorrow, eh? Take these.'

She snatched the two letters as though he might sink his teeth into her hand and just about ran from the office. Edward laughed, but what was there to laugh at? The niggling something was Lumley saying Miss Goldman had finally admitted Edward was last in the office that night. *Finally admitted*. What did that mean? Had Miss Goldman made things look bad by first denying it? Denying it several times, perhaps, too vehemently?

On the way home Edward saw Miss Goldman under torture by Lindsay's secret agents, headed by the plodding Lumley. Miss Goldman's big black eyes wide and staring, drenched in terror, but maybe having a hint of titillated anticipation.

Sibyl was in and ready with loving welcome, for once not absent-minded. In a way watchful, with the sort of smile poised to vanish. He had two gins before dinner.

During the meal, some kind of baked arrangement with pork and prunes in it, he kept catching her eyes and the wondering expression in them. The cats sat about looking plaintive and hard-done-by.

'This is good,' Edward said.

'Yes, isn't it, darling?' Sibyl sounded relieved. 'I've had it on the agenda for simply *ages* and only just got around to it. It's out of a book.'

Edward had a second helping and a lot more broad beans.

Sibyl laughed. 'You seem to have found your appetite again.'

'Who could resist grub like this?'

'Everyone's saying how *thin* you've got. Even Diana said so.'

Bitch. '*Even* Diana?'

'Well, I mean – we haven't seen much of her, that's all I meant, hardly ever.'

Bloody Diana. Ringing up all day long behind his back. Edward sat back and lit a cigarette. Sibyl stared.

'You're *smoking.*'

'So I am. Got a couple of spare throwouts in the way of ashtrays?'

'Of course, darling – but *why?*'

'Why not?' He smiled. 'Self-defence, shall we say?'

Sibyl smiled too but the wary look was back.

Later, after he'd done the day's dishes, Edward chose a round brown and a square greyish from Sibyl's offerings.

'You're funny tonight,' Sibyl said.

'Funny how?'

'Well, *smoking* – and saying *grub.* You *never* say grub.'

Edward grabbed her in a hug so hard Sibyl squealed. 'Grub, grub, grub,' he sang, 'remember what Emerson said.'

'Darling, you're *hurting.*'

He released her. 'You can blame your body-building

grub.' He grinned as he left the living-room. He started up the stairs.

Sibyl followed him out. 'Consistency is one of the things I *love* you for,' she called up after him.

Edward blew her a kiss.

The ashtrays looked fine in his room.

Next day during his lunch hour, with a strange sensation it was something he couldn't evade or even postpone, he bought three enormous floor cushions in eyestrain colours and a couple of bucket chairs in plastic, purple and acid green respectively. To give his room the blast it needed.

CHAPTER XV

A clean, large, light room. Edward enters, strong, debonair. Rachel smiles a welcome. Edward tells her their programme entails travel. Rachel delighted. He tells her they'll hop about all over, with young Edward. He knows Rachel is thanatotic. Edward will save her from herself. Rachel attempts disguise of the suicidal thing with lots of happy gabbling and —

'Mr Piper?'

Edward focused on Lumley seated opposite.

'I asked why you dislike Miss Lucas?'

Respite from Lumley yesterday, now here he was again. 'I don't dislike her.'

Lumley consulted his notebook. 'On Monday you said "I don't like her".'

'I meant in relation to my wife. They were sharing a flat at the time. One thought of them together and saw the difference. I mean I fell in love with Sibyl but not with Diana.'

'I see.'

It was Diana had put Lumley on to him. He'd got rid

of Lindsay's pressure but a worse had started with Lumley. Because Lindsay was part of it, still alive, with his derisive smile.

'Miss Goldman also admits that Mr Reid called in here to the office quite a few times, and phoned as often.'

'Naturally.' Edward leaned back, lit a cigarette and smiled through the smoke. 'We were working together on a film.'

'Would that be the film Miss Lucas told me about?'

What had the bitch said?

'That you denied on Monday when you said your only contact with Mr Reid was in regard to taxation matters?'

'Well, he didn't want it known, he asked me to keep mum about it – I see now it doesn't matter.'

'So you saw Mr Reid frequently?'

'More like now and again. Remember I'm a nine-to-fiver.'

Lumley smiled in sympathy.

Edward said, 'After ideas, mostly. He wasn't much good at ideas, had to scratch around.'

'He seems well known in his field.'

'He was successful, I grant you that,' Edward said, 'but it was all hack stuff. Envied me of all people, guessed I had the knack. Felt sorry for him, asked him to have a go at an idea I had – hence the film.'

'I see.'

Edward wished Lumley had some mannerism. He was a still man. No twitchings, not an eyebrow-rubber or ear-puller, no pipe and matches to fiddle with.

'Miss Lucas is very fond of your wife and very much admires her ceramics.'

Oh yes, *very*. Edward smiled.

'Your wife has a pottery at home?'

'I'm sure Miss Lucas told you. It's why we live out in the backblocks.'

Lumley nodded.

'I'd never choose to live there myself,' Edward went on, 'but love conquers all, they say.' He grinned. 'She had a great old chase landing me, had some quite stiff competition, poor old girl.'

Lumley had an encouraging smile.

'She thought being a potter would somehow carry weight with me being a writer.'

'So you *are* a writer.'

'Knackwise.' He went on staring into Lumley's eyes. He felt all at once pleased with the way things were going. It seemed to him he and Lumley shared equal enjoyment in these meetings. They might become a regular thing. He liked Lumley, Lumley liked him, together they were engaged in a pleasurable analysis of some obscure situation that had to do with poor old bloody Lindsay. Edward felt neither aggressive nor abject. Lumley had sought him out for the keenness of his observation, that's all. Just the way Lindsay had. Lumley too was concerned for ecological balance, with the wit to see behind Edward's tax man's façade to his real genius.

'Did Mr Reid seem at all worried lately?' Lumley asked.

'Yes, matter of fact. I think he'd got himself in deep over some bloke's wife. Played pretty fast and loose. Owed a lot of money around too. Paid me back some last week though Christ knows I didn't press the old boy.'

'Last week?'

Edward blinked.

Lumley didn't even have to consult his notebook. 'You said you hadn't seen Reid that week.'

'I'm sorry, I thought I hadn't, one loses track, I thought that was the week he was away.' The error confused him. He wanted to be fair and square with Lumley. Lumley was a nice man. Edward felt muddled.

'Mr Reid was murdered on Tuesday last week, December 9th. Is that the day you saw him, the occasion he repaid the money he owed you?'

'No,' Edward said, 'no. It must have been the Monday.'
He wished Lumley wouldn't say murdered. He groped at
a memory. 'It must have been, Monday's the day he
phoned, I'm sure Miss Goldman would know.'

'Here or at his place?'

'In a pub. Yes, I remember now, in a pub, he drank a
lot.'

'Which hotel would that be?'

'It might have been two or three, it usually was, we often
did that.'

'You often did that.' It was just a statement in Lumley's
gentle voice, just a repetition of Edward's words.

Without warning a feeling of terror shook Edward. Beneath the desk he ground his hands together.

Lumley missed nothing. 'Are you all right, Mr Piper?'

'Yes. Yes, thank you.' It was a swift vision of Lumley's
mind that terrified Edward. He'd seen inside it, as though
by X-ray, to neat columns of dates and times and truths
and lies; meticulous, tidy, as orderly as his own. Far more
orderly.

Lumley pursued the slip as Edward had known he would.
'You said you saw Mr Reid only now and again. Just what
do you mean by often, Mr Piper?'

'Well,' Edward tried a smile, tried to steady his voice,
'my life may seem pretty routine but it's very busy, a tight
schedule, I suppose it's that, I suppose something that
happens occasionally seems like often if it comes round too
quickly interrupting one's work programme.'

'I know what you mean,' Lumley said. He sounded sym-
pathetic again. Edward sighed. The feeling of mutual ex-
ploration had vanished. He must stay on guard even with
Lumley. Especially with Lumley.

Lumley looked in his notebook. 'You knew, of course,
Mr Reid had just been commissioned to write the film
of a popular book.'

'No. No, I didn't know.' No seemed best to everything.

Besides, it sounded like a trick non-question.

'Miss Lucas told me about it. Mr Reid regarded it as the pinnacle of his career.' He paused. His eyes didn't budge from Edward's. 'He didn't tell you?'

'No. I wasn't among his cronies. I thought I'd made that clear.'

'Yes. Miss Lucas stated that Mr Reid said he would be forced to cancel the story he was working on with you.'

Edward shrugged. 'Hardly working. A few brief chats. Nothing serious. He was busy on a series of television plays.'

'Yes.' Lumley consulted his notebook again, but Edward knew now Lumley had no need, the notebook was one of his tricks. Edward lit a cigarette he didn't want.

Lindsay's death was unintended. Edward was sure of this. Then why did he feel so guilty? It was Lumley's persistence, Lumley prodded by Diana. It wasn't Lindsay dying. It was hard sometimes to believe Lindsay was dead. Sometimes alone in the office, when the telephone rang, he expected to hear Lindsay's 'Look, old boy'. Or when the door opened he looked up for Lindsay breezing in. Sometimes he knew Lindsay was still alive, that this was all a test of him they'd concocted, Lindsay the instigator, experimenting in real life for a scene in his third play.

Lindsay pleads, a little toad twisted with envy. Edward has the taunting smile. He winks at Brian. Brian gets the message. Edward is sauntering in and out of night spots. Girls throw themselves at him. Boys too. He picks a short girl, thin and small-boned, black hair flopping over alert black eyes. Lumley watches from the shadows.

'The murderer left us *some* fingerprints.' Lumley was smiling at him.

'Oh. Did he? I thought you said – '

'Plenty of Mr Reid's around, plus others, the natural amount. It was the total removal in specific places – that was the blunder he made.'

'Blunder? You mean you've got him?' Under Lumley's encouraging smile Edward felt like a child straining for the right answer. 'He left a couple? Or she?'

'None at all.' Lumley looked puzzlingly pleased. 'But it was only the desk, two chairs, around the handles of three doors, and just one glass among a number of used glasses in the kitchen. All wiped clean of fingerprints. What d'you make of that, Mr Piper, as a writer?'

'I don't know what to make of it, I know nothing of fingerprints.'

'It sheds light on a number of things. I think we can safely assume it was someone who had a drink with Mr Reid, who sat at his desk with him, who was known to Mr Reid and made welcome as a friend or associate. Most importantly it reveals character, idiosyncracies.'

Edward stubbed out his cigarette. Lumley had nothing, just tidiness. That was nothing to go on. Edward brushed some specks of ash from his desk and realigned the ashtray with his desk calendar the way he liked it.

'Thank you, Mr Piper, you've been very helpful.' Lumley got up with his nice smile and notebook. 'Good morning – no, don't get up.'

Edward wasn't getting up. His legs would give way. He watched Lumley go out and shut the door.

He looked at his desk. Work was impossible, the thought of it bewildering. He opened a file and stared at the top page, at the meaningless jumble of words and figures. All he could see, with dreadful clarity, was the precise listing in Lumley's head. Sooner or later Lumley would re-order the list into a logical sequence. He needed a few more facts, a few more lies to establish them. With Diana's help. Diana was keeping Lumley's nose pointed at Edward. Diana had discounted random thuggery, Diana said it was someone Lindsay knew. She'd probably wept on Lumley's chest along with some other sly touches of feminine flapdoodle. Lumley had fallen for it. But why should

Diana be so vindictive? Edward had done her no injury so why this dead set against him? She'd taken against him at the start, didn't want Sibyl to marry him, but that was all old stuff. Had Lindsay instilled the idea? Was it something picked up from Lindsay's contempt for him, jelling after Lindsay's death? Lindsay had amused Diana with the continuing story of Edward's bumbling progress on the script, told in his racy sardonic style, making a serial of it to keep Diana in stitches. Edward could hear Lindsay's withering recital, and the final slur: 'Hasn't a clue, bloody little envious toad.' Lindsay's death had turned Diana's amusement to animosity, made her knowledge grist to Lumley and perilous to Edward. Clever little Diana had come up with Edward's motive: the fact that Lindsay had ditched him because of the new commission. It wasn't a motive for murder. People had disappointments all the time. Lots of things made lots of people angry. They might strike out, some of them, but not to kill. Edward had struck out on one of his rare silly impulses, but not to kill. The ungoverned moment had gone so fast he couldn't even remember it. He wasn't a killer. He was the mildest of men. And there wasn't a shred of the sort of evidence Lumley needed. No fingerprints, eyewitnesses, bullets, bloody knives. He was safe as houses.

Edward stared round his office. It seemed to have shrunk suddenly. Here is my space.

In any case, Edward had denied knowledge of Lindsay's new commission and the scrapping of the ecology film. He'd been clever. He was a match for Diana. And for Lumley. Did Lumley hope to wear him down? Two could play at that little game.

Mr Strachan came through on the intercom: he'd like a word with Mr Piper when Mr Piper was free.

Edward went at once so he wouldn't have time to worry about the reason, which might well be some client's muddled affairs.

It wasn't. Mr Strachan wasn't smiling. He didn't ask Edward to sit down. 'Well, Mr Piper, this fellow going to take much longer, this detective fellow?'

Edward smiled. 'I think he's just about finished, Mr Strachan.'

'Let's hope so. It's not so much the time, though that's a consideration. It's the disturbance to the staff, they're noticing, you see. This sort of thing starts talk, it's bound to, however discreet the fellow is. There's the office party on Friday, I'd like it ended before then. It's come to my ears he's questioned Miss Goldman, you see, possibly others. And now if you please he wants to see the cleaners.'

Edward felt the old panic of insecurity. Supposing he lost his job? If it looked like coming to that the best he could do would be to resign before the blow fell. Live off Sibyl's pots and Daddy.

'Is there something amusing, Mr Piper?'

'No, of course not, sir.'

'I'm surprised Mr Reid's character takes such a lot of analysing.'

'You know the police – '

'No, Mr Piper, I don't.'

'Every little thing, over and over repeatedly.'

Mr Strachan gave him a pale thin look. 'All right, Mr Piper, we'll see.'

That was that, no thank you, just a dismissive bending of his head to the single sheet of paper which was all there ever seemed to be on his desk.

Edward went to lunch then, half an hour earlier than usual. He wasn't hungry. He went into a pub for a gin and tonic, but asked instead for whisky. He had a second whisky. What did Lumley want with the cleaners?

He'd meant to keep up with the News. Every night he missed it with all its ecological disasters. Missed it on purpose. The same with newspapers which he carried around unopened. He imagined men sitting in sinister conclave hatching plots against the environment. Men with Diana's face, with Lindsay's arrogant smile. Nice-seeming men like Lumley.

Why should Lumley want to see the cleaners? They didn't hoard waste paper. What could the cleaners know? Only what Lumley already knew from Miss Goldman, that Lindsay popped into the office sometimes. The cleaners couldn't have seen Lindsay more than once, even then perhaps only one cleaner. Wouldn't remember, anyway; not interested. Lindsay could have been a client on a late call. In fact Lindsay *was* a client. There was nothing in the cleaners for Lumley. But there was something for Mr Strachan, whose head must be gradually filling with whispered absurdities.

Edward must stop Lumley coming to the office. Tell Lumley he'd gladly meet him anywhere but the office. It was a reasonable request to make, Lumley would understand about office gossip.

The clouds were low and full of a long threat. Humidity had drained all colours to a wet grey. Edward with a cigarette pushed through the Christmas crowds. The whisky had left a rotten Lindsayish taste. Shop windows were full of bright deceptive Christmas packaging. He waited for the green at an intersection and crossed in a jam of bare limbs sticky with sweat. He passed a window full of cheap furniture, mahogany-type, sale-priced in fluorescence. He thought of Sibyl's hair : chestnut-type. Out They Go, Bottom Prices.

Had they anything in common? Ever, had they? He remembered her insensitive overriding of all his wishes. All along they'd done what Sibyl wanted. Her over-pitched underlined voice shouting his down. Relentlessly selfish. He'd had the same problem with Lindsay. Perhaps Edward had a knack for getting along with people he couldn't get along with. It was his reticence that let them have all the say, get away all the time with their own way.

He gave Miss Goldman his nicest smile on the way in. Miss Goldman had always liked him. She smiled back. She had a sort of worried look.

He got out Pittwater and Hartog and worked mechanically.

Sibyl had no taste. All these years a woman of no taste. No discretion. Babbling out everything to Lumley, a simple, plodding man Edward could handle on his ear. A nice man fundamentally; inclined to pounce but only because of his job. A nice sort of character for Edward's thing: a plodding, unimaginative, clumsy minor cog.

The afternoon passed quietly, as office afternoons should. And always had. He ran over Lumley's morning visit. Summed up, he thought they'd got on well together. Lumley had to go through the motions, but Edward thought Lumley appreciated the quality of his intelligence. It was a very long afternoon, full of Pittwater and Hartog.

CHAPTER XVI

He got home in a temper. Mr Strachan's thin icy warning nagged at him. Lumley's persistence terrified. Lumley's stupid persistence was alarming to Mr Strachan, whose staff were colourless cogs in his precious business. The heavy traffic, teeming rain, damn-fool pedestrians smothered him. Twice he braked so the seat-belt wrenched at his chest. Far back somewhere in his mind he thought the session with Lumley had gone well, but Edward was angry that the sessions should continue at all. Diana was stoking the fire out of pure malice, but that would run itself out and Lumley's visits would stop. Edward would outlast them because his life was at stake. His simple, inoffensive life lived in the background. It was all he had. And more substantial, more durable, than Lumley's silly trick questions. He knew this even while the accumulation of pressures drew a tight knot strangling thought. Strangling all thought of his creative work. Keeping him from it.

Cooking smells came from the kitchen but Sibyl was in the living-room. He glowered at her from the doorway, his temper simmering like her saucepans.

Sibyl looked up from the big bluey-grey jug she was holding in her lap on her frilly settee. She looked grubby, a dirty sleeveless top and dirty brief shorts. 'It's been a bad firing day, sugar – sorry, I mean darling. The glaze just went all *wrong*.'

From where Edward stood it looked no different from any, repulsive as all her work. He moved slowly and sat heavily in an armchair, swiping the ashtray on its arm in the direction of Sibyl's tiled hearth, where it broke. He hadn't meant to do that, had he?

Sibyl looked startled. Then she said, 'Never mind, it's only a second.'

'Like me.'

She gave him a quick look, then smiled. She thought he was joking. It was his mild voice. Edward got up, walked slowly to the mantelpiece and picked up her best piece (she said) which she'd stuck between Mummy's vases. He let it fall on to Sibyl's precious tiles with smashing results. He turned his head to see the effect.

Sibyl had jumped up, still holding the jug, shocked, but more angry than frightened. '*My prize pot!*'

'What prize?'

'My *best* – you know what I mean.'

'If that's your best you ought to give it up.'

'You're *insane*.'

Edward walked from the room, churning inside. Sibyl ran after him.

'I'm sorry, darling, I didn't mean that, I only meant when you can't control an impulse.'

Edward walked away from her, back into the living-room. He went to the mantelpiece, picked up Mummy's vases, one in each hand, and hurled them with force down on to the tiles. He knew she'd followed and turned to look at her. She looked bewildered, and silly holding the jug protectively against her chest.

'You wanted me to throw something.'

Sibyl started to cry, a sort of miserable drizzle. Edward left her to it and ran upstairs, feeling puffed at the top, heart pounding. He unlocked his door and slammed it shut behind him. He flung off his tie and jacket and dropped on the divan.

He felt pooped. He felt like he'd just finished an epic. He noticed he was beginning to think like his script was written. That was good. That was the rock Lindsay got hung up on. Lindsay reckoned a high-flown subject demanded high-flown language to put it across. Bloody fool. Grunts were great, the populace understood grunts, the great uncultivated masses felt at home with grunts. Poetic stuff was a dead duck. Poor old Lindsay, way off beam.

His head throbbed with pain. A terrible shame swamped him for the smashing he'd done. Violence didn't suit him, didn't come easily to him. Violence didn't do any good, it achieved nothing. Poor old Sibyl, a bad firing day and then his senseless destruction. He'd like to expunge the episode. He'd apologize, but it would always remain, something done that couldn't be undone. Shame stifled.

Stifled too because he'd written nothing; his work wasn't even begun. Lindsay was to have shown him the ropes but all Lindsay had done was set Edward little projects so he could sneer at them. Ecologically, plantwise, they were a consociation, with the Lindsay species dominant, the Edward species on the bottom rung of the ladder, one of the lowly worts.

Had Lindsay ever intended the ecology thing seriously? Edward could never know now with certainty. And if

Lindsay had he would never have allowed Edward to play any meaningful part in it. None of the kudos. Just a hard slog of research, with Lindsay picking his brain, and through his, Sibyl's. In the animal strata Edward, in Lindsay's view, was the lowest, something Lindsay gobbled up for sustenance and energy. Lindsay at the top, on top, the one with the skill and strength to defeat all comers. Spiders eat flies, small birds eat spiders, larger birds eat smaller birds, Lindsay eats Edward.

There was a knocking on the door and a voice sounding like Sibyl's. After a while they stopped.

Lindsay and those like him stayed at the top, guarding their domain, jealous of it, scaring or killing off competition, reducing rivalry among themselves by sharing out the plummy jobs. Edward's status at Lindsay's level was nil. Edward had no status, he was a parasite, his specialization to protect Lindsay taxwise.

Well, Lindsay had fallen flat on his face. His skill had failed him. Nature had been overbalanced. Poor old bloody Lindsay had been too clever by half. He could see Lindsay's desk like on a film, a close shot with the action completed and the following sequence not yet begun. The big square green glass ashtray he'd cleaned. The other things that were so always there they passed unnoticed. Yet not Lindsay's glass. But it must have been there. They'd both had a drink, there was never a drink going that Lindsay wasn't in on. But Edward had taken only his own glass out to Lindsay's kitchen. During the cleaning-up – he'd done a lot of that – and he remembered distinctly his own glass he'd taken out to the kitchen, one tree in a forest. It didn't matter about Lindsay's glass, the not remembering was the dangerous thing. Already Lumley was setting traps for his memory, thinking it a chink in his armour.

Had Sibyl turned off the waterworks yet? The poor girl seemed on edge.

It wasn't fair of Lumley to question the cleaners. What

could the cleaners tell him? The greater the circle of people Lumley prodded the more talk there'd be. It was this that worried poor old Strachan. Poor old Strachan had been pretty bloody nasty with all that crap about this sort of thing starting talk. His manner had dripped icicles. Christ! Edward got up from the divan, feeling suffocated. He lit a cigarette.

Bloody Lumley and that bitch Diana, even Sibyl wary when he came a bit close like he was going to crack her bloody skull open – all bloody crowding in, Christ, you had to have peace, writing was bloody hard work.

He put the rotten cigarette out in the round brown. He sat at the desk.

Sibyl would regale everyone with every bloody move, he could just hear the bitch, dine out on it for months, all that bloody mob in the living-room. There wasn't a hope in hell Strachan would stick by him, and bloody Wykeham would have a bloody fit. Then the parents –

'Darling, you all right?'

Edward got up and opened the door. 'I'm fine.' He smiled at her.

She looked at his bare desk. 'What do you *do* in here?'

'You'd be surprised.' He kept the smile.

'I hoped you'd come down and join me in a long icy drink.'

'Love to, just the weather for it.'

In the kitchen Sibyl did Campari and soda with ice cubes and lemon slices. Edward stood and watched her. How quick she was with her hands. She looked cleaned-up and nice in a long sleeveless grey sort of thing with tiny pink flowers all over it.

'Sibyl.'

She went still and looked at him.

'I suppose the parents know, I suppose you tell them every move.'

She rushed at him. 'Of *course* not, darling, what a

thing to say.' Her arms squeezed round him tight. 'Is *that* what's driving you crazy? As if I *would*. Besides, tell them what? – I don't know what you mean by *every move*.'

He hugged her close and kissed her hair.

'I cleaned it all up,' Sibyl murmured into his neck, 'the breakages. If Mummy misses the nasties I'll say *I* did it.'

'I'm sorry, darling,' Edward said, his voice husky, 'damn awful traffic and the rain.'

'I know, I know, darling, *everyone*'s on edge with the weather.' She drew her head back and looked at him. 'Aren't you hungry? I turned it all off but it won't take a moment to turn it all on again.'

The kitchen looked too long-used by grubby hands. 'Had a big lunch,' Edward said, feeling hollow, 'how about you?' He moved from her and sat down at the table.

'Matter of fact I had some, you know *me*. How's the drink, want another?'

'No, thanks – yes, why not?'

Sibyl laughed and replenished their drinks. She sat down opposite him. A cat watching for the opportunity at once jumped on to her lap. It was always Sibyl's lap, never Edward's. Sibyl fondled the cat.

'Darling, what *is* worrying you? Let's have it out. I can't *bear* to see you like this, getting thin – and everything.'

Edward sighed.

'It can't be just the weather.'

'It's my creative work I can't get at.'

Sibyl stared. 'What creative work?' Then at the look on his face she added in a rush, 'I mean isn't that all over now Lindsay's dead? I mean, darling, you've never said anything before except when we first met and you said then about your *ambition* to write but you've never done anything *about* it, you haven't even *mentioned* it till this Lindsay business came up.'

Edward stared at the table.

'Well, *have* you?'

'There's been no time, no place, no quiet.'

Sibyl was silent. He looked at her. She said, 'I think that's just excuses – no, darling, I don't mean it's not true but I think if you'd really *meant* to you'd have done it *somehow*. Don't *you – really and truly*?'

'I expect you're right as always.'

'I thought it was all over now Lindsay's dead.'

Edward swallowed most of his drink.

'And it was a big relief,' Sibyl said.

'Lindsay's death?' He stared at her.

'You know very well what I mean – ever since he mentioned the wretched thing you've been funny so how can I help being glad you're rid of him?'

Rid of him?

'Especially as he never appreciated you. Diana says Lindsay called you a bloody pest.'

'When?'

'Oh – various times. Don't forget we've been friends ever since school. He was even going to switch to another tax man.'

'She was jealous, she's being malicious.'

'But Diana isn't *like* that.'

A suspicion struck Edward. 'She's been out here?'

'Well, yes, darling, a couple of times during the day. She's turned to me a lot since he – since it happened.'

Bloody bitches, nattering, twisting, concocting. Keeping Lindsay alive.

'Darling, come down the coast for Christmas, forget it all. D'you realize it's Christmas Day tomorrow week?'

The idea tempted. But what might Lumley find out during his absence? Lumley egged on by Diana? 'What about the cats?' he said.

'Nance'll pop in and feed them, I've lined her up already, it's much better for them to stay in familiar surroundings.'

Sibyl meant to get her own way again, taking it for

granted. 'Have you done anything yet about the cock-roaches?'

Sibyl did her bewildered laugh. 'This craziness about cockroaches, darling, there *aren't* any, they're all round about the harbour, *miles* from us.'

Edward knew better. This sort of weather, humidity, all structures, all textures, soggy with rain. Ecologically, cockroaches were tough and supremely adaptable; they'd be on the earth long after humanity was gone. If humanity left any earth.

'And Christmas, darling?'

'Just don't hold me to a promise I haven't made.'

'You look so terribly *tired.*'

Just then Edward remembered his growing script, and smiled. He reached across the table and took her hand. He saw the cat's head was flecked with Sibyl's ash. He imagined Sibyl's astonishment when the script would be done. It would be something accomplished. Sibyl was squeezing his hand with a sort of urgency.

'Darling,' she said. Then said, 'I *do* love you, Edward.'

'Me too.'

'D'you think – will you – I mean tonight, darling, *don't* let me sleep alone tonight? Please?'

A surge of emotion choked him. He stumbled round the table, enveloped her in a hug. The outraged cat jumped down. Sibyl turned her face up to his. They kissed. Darling Sibyl, his darling Sibyl who'd transformed his life. He loved her, he truly loved her. He felt a sob in his throat. He buried his face in her hair to hide the tears.

'Darling, darling, darling,' Sibyl said over and over into his chest.

It was like old times. Darling Sibyl. It was like old times, after a shower, slipping into Sibyl's bed, the swoony kiss, her hands all over him, caressing, imploring. Like old times until again, still, he couldn't.

'Darling, never mind, don't try so hard, you're overtired, go to sleep, darling.'

Edward cried.

'Darling, please, please don't.' Sibyl's left arm framed his head and her tears mingled with his. Her agony of sympathy was convulsive.

It was Lumley. Lumley and Lindsay. Lindsay and Diana. Himself and Lindsay. It was himself and his crime. There, he admitted it : crime. His crime had castrated his life and his body. The tears were for all of it.

They stayed in each other's arms. Edward pretended sleep to stop Sibyl's anguish. At last he felt her relax, felt her impetus slip away into sleep. Then the breathing like the filing of rusty iron. In bed with Sibyl, but no more bliss. Never again, no more ever.

His mind went back to the kitchen. Cockroaches. And Sibyl's protest the wrong way round. 'Tell them what?' she'd said, but saying first, with too many stresses, 'Of course not, darling, as if I *would*.' Betraying her own suspicions, fed by Diana.

No bliss, but a dream of cockroaches. Great shuddery, sly, quick things all over him, the bed, everything, everywhere. He woke in a sweat. Christ! All the crap!

CHAPTER XVII

Edward stared at Lumley's empty chair. Lumley had left the office. 'Back in a moment,' he'd said. Lumley had phoned this morning and asked might he pop in for a few moments. Edward almost panicked, seeing Lumley and Mr Strachan tangle in the corridor, hearing the freeze of Mr Strachan's dismissal. Strachan would give him the sack. At once he asked Lumley, although fear made his voice peremptory, if they might meet somewhere else. Lumley agreed, courteous as always. Lumley knew why, he didn't have to be told.

This was an office, Lumley's or somebody else's, a grubby, bare sort of room. Rain at the dirty windows. A room Lumley's questions would be worse in. A room where Lumley's insinuating deductions would lower Edward's morale. But safe at least from Strachan's eyes.

Lumley every day. A week to Christmas. Caught between Lumley and the parents on a rack of tormenting questions.

He wanted life with Sibyl to go on. Wanted it desperately. He wanted to go on making love to her. When he looked back to their life as it had been, before Lindsay spoiled everything by dying, he saw it as ideal, himself the noble creative husband, Sibyl the loving helpful wife, their son – but they had no son. Edward frowned. He was muddled again. It was having Lumley round his neck.

She was worse now without their lovemaking, now that he couldn't. More casual, it seemed to him, more upsetting, more thoughtless. Resentful and contemptuous. Last night, for instance, after a Lumley day. He'd tried in her bed before the cockroaches, she'd seemed so sweet, forbearing, compliant yet deliciously active. So understanding when he cried. Then this morning going out of her way to upset him. With a distant, cold manner. Sibyl knew he wanted every evening free to work on Edward's thing. So she organized a meeting in the house for Friday night, tomorrow. Deliberately. Just to get back at him. Just because some agitator phoned news of some new outrage sprung by the local council, or maybe the State government. Something to do with a road. Or perhaps a house. In the middle of Edward's breakfast on the kitchen extension. So that he was too suffocated to eat, and no food yesterday. It had to be their house because others had sleeping children or old folk watching telly or sickness or repairs or extensions going on.

'We'll have it here,' Sibyl told the phone, 'you tell the

Spensers and Ramsays and I'll get the Cliffords and all the Joneses.'

Knowing he wanted to work and the noise would get in his brain, knowing he'd hear their voices even though he couldn't. So in between phone calls Edward reminded her of his work.

'I know, darling,' Sibyl said dialling, 'I know you *say* that but this is *important*.'

'So is this,' he said.

'Gosh,' she stopped before the last digit, 'you can write any old time, these people *care* about things,' and completed the call. As if he were an annoying or meaningless stranger. Their life together a nothing, their love subservient to sewerage or kerbing. He hated the way she talked. The vulgarity of it. The idiotic underlinings.

'I thought we'd done with meetings for this year.' He got up from the table.

'We *have*, this is just an *emergency*. Besides, *what* writing?'

He'd left then. The cats unmoved at seeing him go.

What trick was Lumley playing by making him wait, letting him stew? Hoping for nervy errors?

Tomorrow was the office party. Strachan expected him there, would watch for him, make it a test. Edward couldn't face it. Trapped between the office party and Sibyl's meeting.

Lumley came in with his pleasant smile. 'Sorry,' he said, 'one gets caught up.' He sat down facing Edward. Out of a drawer he got some foolscap pages, clipped together. Was that himself, Edward wondered, typed up from the notebook? Lumley ran through the pages, then looked at Edward. 'They won't miss you at the office?'

'No, that's arranged.'

'You businessmen, always a cover story.' Lumley seemed in a good mood and looked somehow more nourished.

Edward smiled back at the tired old joke. Lumley pushed

the foolscap pages aside. Edward tried not to look at them. He lit a cigarette. He hoped Lumley would clear up the matter of the cleaners so Mr Strachan would have one less thing to carp about.

'Mr Strachan not worried, is he?' Lumley said.

'Not worried, no. He did think your visits might start talk, he seemed upset that you wanted to see the cleaners.'

'Well, that's over with, nothing to it. I've seen the ladies. In their eyes you're tops, Mr Piper, the only real gentleman in the office. That please you?'

'Well – naturally.'

'They say you're often last to leave. One lady recognized Mr Reid from his photograph, said she'd seen him now and again.'

'That's hardly surprising.'

'Exactly. He was a client of yours.' Lumley's smile today had an extra warmth. 'I don't think there's much more, Mr Piper.'

Let's get it over with, Edward thought. He was on tenterhooks. Then he thought, a laugh bubbling, he'd tell Sibyl about Lumley's 'ladies'. Then knew he couldn't tell Sibyl. It would be Lumley, not the silly outmoded term, Sibyl would be shocked at. Sibyl mustn't know about Edward's Lumley connection.

'Mrs Fleming,' Lumley said straight out of his head. Edward waited, tense.

'Says you signed a couple of letters with Mr Reid's name.'

'I explained to her how it happened.'

'Yes. She thought no more of it until later when you became, as Mrs Fleming put it, like a different person.'

Edward laughed. 'You don't know Mrs Fleming, drives us all crazy with her fussing. We all tease her.'

'I see.' Lumley looked amused. 'People like that you feel sometimes you'd like to put a bomb under.'

'A bit drastic, but that's the feeling.'

Lumley put the foolscap pages away in the drawer. He leaned back in his chair and smiled at Edward. 'I see you've started smoking.'

'Any law against it?' Edward stubbed out his cigarette, pleased with his casual reaction.

Lumley went on watching him with his nice face in his glasses.

'Anything else?' Edward asked in his mild, tolerant voice.

'Nothing new.' Lumley got out the notebook and glanced through it.

Edward sighed with relief. He felt they were getting somewhere, getting to the end. He believed Lumley felt the same. Together they'd thrash the thing out, toss it around, then Lumley could file it away with other unsolved cases. Lumley was frowning at the notebook. Edward wanted to see the frown go, wanted to help Lumley with whatever was troubling him. He wondered was Lumley being diddled taxwise. Perhaps he could help there too when Lumley had this other business sorted out. Lumley could replace that bloody creep Lindsay as his client. There wouldn't be all that crappy muddle Lindsay's finances had.

Lumley shut the notebook. 'No, nothing new.'

'That's great, old boy,' Edward said.

Lumley gave him a look, quizzical, but a bit wary like the look he'd got from Sibyl lately. Then Lumley said, 'Mrs Fleming mentioned your starting smoking.'

'Busybody,' Edward said.

'Because you've always railed against it so, she said.'

'Mrs Fleming can go fry her face.'

'And your language shocked her – not like Mr Piper at all, she said.'

Edward had had enough of Mrs Fleming. 'I can't see what you're getting at. Have Mrs Fleming's biases any bearing on Mr Reid's – on the case?'

Lumley consulted the notebook. 'You said the first time I saw you – that was on December 11th, two days after

Mr Reid's murder – that you hadn't seen him since the week before the previous one.'

'I thought we cleared that up.' Edward felt a hollowness inside.

'Then on December 17th you said he paid back some money he owed you the week before.'

'Yes, I told you, I got muddled, one week's pretty much like another, I made a mistake of a week.'

'Two weeks,' Lumley said.

Edward got a cigarette out, then wished he hadn't because his fingers shook so and Lumley missed nothing.

'You finally suggested it was the Monday you saw Mr Reid, Monday, December 8th, the day before he was murdered.'

'Yes, it must have been, he phoned, I hoped you'd check with Miss Goldman.'

'You didn't like Mr Reid.'

'He was my friend.' It was Lumley's statements Edward didn't like. They weren't questions. Lumley made them sound like rigid beliefs, like Mrs Fleming's ingrained prejudices.

'On Monday, December 15th, six days after Mr Reid's death, you said he didn't impress you as a likeable man.'

Edward lit his cigarette.

'A bit cocky, you said, a know-all.' Lumley had a trap to spring, it was in his eyes behind the glasses.

Edward waited.

'Boasted about his women, you said, in a tiresome manner.'

'We were still friends, he was my only friend, we'd been friends for years.'

'You said Mr Reid consulted you only about taxation matters. You said that on the same day, December 15th, insisting that Miss Lucas was mistaken about your collaborating with Mr Reid on a film story.'

'I thought we'd cleared up these points – they're only

trifles, aren't they?'

'Trifles, inconsistencies, dodges – there are many terms, Mr Piper.' Lumley surprisingly smiled. Edward felt a fraction safer.

'I admit I got a bit flummoxed, I was so upset at the news, I haven't got over it yet.'

'I see, yes. Mr Reid was a hack writer, you said – does that mean not very bright, not very original?'

'Well, yes.' Edward tapped his ash at the floor. 'Run of the mill.'

'But he was successful.'

'Yes.'

'And that's why you asked him to help develop an idea you had?'

Lumley was leading up to something again. Edward wished he could remember what he'd said, wished he had that cursed notebook in Lumley's hands. 'Yes.'

'He agreed because he knew you had the knack.'

Edward felt his face flush and cursed that too. 'Yes, I suppose that was it.'

'Miss Lucas says it was the other way round.'

'I can't help what Miss Lucas says. Naturally she'd say that, being one of his – one of his – ' He must try to remain calm.

'Miss Lucas says Mr Reid had been thinking for some time about an ecology film from a human interest angle.'

'Nude lovers.' Edward laughed.

'And that his only purpose in approaching you was to stop you pestering him.'

'Bloody little toad.'

'He hoped it would keep you quiet while he finished his television plays, at which time he intended to sever his connection with you as his taxation accountant.'

'It's a pack of lies, I hope you realize that. Miss Lucas took a dislike to me right from the start, one of those unreasoning impulses people – women – get. She hated it that Sibyl – my wife – fell like a ton of bricks.'

'I see.'

Lumley didn't see, of course. He'd branded Edward as a liar just on the evidence of a few weak little fibs. Now he disbelieved everything Edward said. If Edward told him the truth about Lindsay, what Lindsay was really like, Lumley would put it down to Edward's lies and envy. He'd thought Lumley would be a fair man, a man after justice. Instead, without a hope of making an arrest, he was devoting all his time at taxpayers' expense to badgering Edward, ruining his life with Sibyl, losing him his job. It was what Diana wanted and Lumley was her pawn.

'I think it's out, Mr Piper.'

Edward took his fingers from the mashed cigarette end in the ashtray. Lumley was smiling at it. For a moment he looked like Lindsay. It was the smile that Edward caught sideways. They had the same initials, that was all. If Edward could think of Lindsay as Reid even that similarity would vanish.

'You don't like Miss Lucas, do you?'

Edward shrugged. 'I've no feeling about Miss Lucas of any kind.'

'On December 17th you told me Mr Reid had seemed worried of late and you thought he might have got involved with another man's wife.'

Edward sighed. Let Lumley ramble on to the end, at least it would be over.

'Miss Lucas states Mr Reid left married women strictly alone.'

'Maybe she's right, she'd know better than I would.'

'Can you think of anything else Mr Reid may have been worried about?'

'I wasn't his confidant.'

'Just his friend.'

'He had hundreds.'

'Miss Lucas denies Mr Reid was worried. He had a

casual attitude to life, he was successful, he did the work he liked doing, he had no money worries.'

'How much longer is this going on?' Edward looked at his watch. 'I should have been back at the office half an hour ago. Is there any purpose anyway, aside from disrupting my entire life?' Anger felt hot inside him.

Lumley said in his gentle voice, 'I'll have a word to Mr Strachan, straighten it out.'

'Better to have done with it altogether,' Edward grated out.

'Absolutely, and so we shall. It's just a matter of following through until we've tied as many loose ends as we can. And you didn't know about Mr Reid's latest commission?'

This was the big question. Lumley threw it away like a nothing, even shifting a bit in his chair as though about to end the interview. Lumley was full of tricks.

'I've already told you, no,' Edward said, 'I've already answered all these questions.'

'Miss Lucas says Mr Reid planned to tell you at once.'

'He didn't tell me,' Edward said. 'Put it down to his casual attitude,' he added, his voice tight with control.

'It seems all the strings came together during his week at Hayman Island. That's when he got the news, Miss Lucas says, upon their return.'

Edward felt sick, but not at the peril he was in. It was life's unfairness, all the plums to Lindsay. It made a gnawing hunger inside him, worse than his hunger for food.

'They returned on the Sunday and he telephoned you on the Monday, Miss Lucas says, the day before he was murdered.'

'He did. I told you. We had a few drinks. He paid back some money he owed me.'

'And that's all?'

'A crappy gift from Hayman, a tie, he gave me that.'

'He didn't tell you the good news he was bursting with?'

'*No, no, no,* how often d'you want me to say it?'

Lumley watched him, still and silent, for a moment that lasted years. 'Miss Lucas says Mr Reid intended to invite you to his flat as soon as possible to settle the matter.'

'Well, he didn't. I remember now he said he was pretty tied up all that week after being away, his play to finish, and he'd contact me later about the ecology thing.'

'You've just remembered that?'

'Yes, we were drinking, he talked a lot, it wasn't worth remembering till now.'

'I see. Miss Lucas says she had theatre tickets for the Tuesday night and Mr Reid regretted he couldn't go with her because of a previous appointment.'

'I can't help the lies they told each other.'

'No. That was Tuesday evening, the evening during which he was murdered.'

Edward almost stopped breathing. 'What was?'

'The appointment Mr Reid had made that prevented his going to the theatre with Miss Lucas.'

'From what I knew of him it was probably some girl he'd picked up.'

'I see, yes. Perhaps he was waiting for her, having a drink by himself. There was just his glass on his desk.'

Edward clenched his hands together between his knees.

'Well, that's all, Mr Piper, thanks very much for your co-operation.' Lumley tucked the notebook in a side pocket and stood up.

Edward's relief was short-lived. He'd just thought of something. If Lumley spoke to Strachan it would put things more wrong than right, put things dead wrong. Nothing would get old Strachan's nose more of a twitch than Lumley smoothing over Edward's absences. He could handle it better himself, keep the old bastard in the dark with gullible

Goldman's help. He stood up.

'I'd rather explain to Mr Strachan myself, if you don't mind.'

'Certainly, Mr Piper.' Lumley smiled as Edward moved to the door. He followed Edward, seemed about to extend his hand but didn't. 'Let's hope there won't be much more of it.'

Edward left without saying goodbye. If he didn't have food he'd faint. It was just on twelve. When he got to the GPO he went in and called Miss Goldman. He'd just left his client, he said, so might as well have an early lunch, and in case anyone was looking for him he'd be back soon after one. Miss Goldman accepted his story without question.

Edward went to Lindsay's bloody good steakhouse. He felt he'd been there a million times instead of only once. He had a thick rump steak rare, salad and two rolls with butter. He also had two double whiskies. Then a brandy with his coffee. A headache started. It was Lumley. Lumley wasn't the discreet and gentle man Edward had thought at their first meeting. He was full of cheap twists and turns, melodramatic bombshells. He knew it all, had all the jigsaw except the final clinching piece. He knew the answers to all his questions but one, and that he hoped to trick out of Edward through fear and worry and fatigue. Maybe he had no feeling about it, didn't care whether Edward was guilty or not. Just nail a culprit, win the battle, make an arrest. Edward hated him. The guilt was Lindsay's. Diana knew this and was out to whitewash Lindsay. Diana made Lindsay out as generous, gifted, long-suffering, honourable. The rotten, weedy little turd. No one knew better than Edward.

The lunch hour girl was in Miss Goldman's place. She smiled at him. He saw no one else. Strachan would be out at his vegetarian restaurant, strictly teetotal.

Edward spread out some work. The headache was worse.

He felt trapped in a tightening circle. He felt stifled. He went to the men's room and took some aspirin. Back at his desk he tried to remember what day it was. Even his desk calendar had no meaning. It had no entries. He didn't put Lumley on his desk calendar.

A tap came on the door and Mr Strachan's head in his stuffy old hat poked round it.

'Oh, you're back, I see.' He came in, silly old fool. Unsmiling, he came over to Edward's desk, still hatted. 'You'll be at the party tomorrow, Mr Piper?'

'Of course, sir.'

'Busy?'

Edward managed a smile. Couldn't the old idiot see for himself?

'Yes, I see you are.' Mr Strachan was staring down at Edward's desk, not at the deceptive spread of open files and folders but at Edward's notepad, at the neat rows of cockroaches that almost filled the page.

It helped with knotty problems. Edward almost said it but couldn't be bothered. Mr Strachan went back to the door.

'We particularly like our seniors to attend the Christmas party, you see. It imparts a sense of the firm's cohesion, it impresses the juniors and does much to keep them in hand.' He sniffed. 'The drink problem.'

'I know, Mr Strachan, you've told me.' Every bloody year.

Mr Strachan gave him a not very friendly look and went out, shutting the door.

Edward tore off the cockroaches and screwed them up tight. He felt this afternoon was a test. If he let go now he'd never get back again. Somehow he must find sense, and most of all a worthwhile meaning, in the jumble of papers spread in front of him. He'd always been a dab hand. It came to him as a shock that he'd actually enjoyed his work.

He threw the ball of paper away and made an effort he thought would be supreme, but as it turned out it was simple enough after all. All he had to do was apply himself. The afternoon passed quickly and Lumley at the end of it was only a silly puppet.

Sibyl was waiting when he got home. 'Darling, darling, I'm sorry, what a *pig* I am.' She hugged him close. 'It really *is* honestly and *truly* the last meeting of all, I think till February, I did *try* to avoid it here but you know – the others all seemed to have such *solid* excuses.'

'It's all right,' Edward said, dismally back in the thick of it, 'what time are they coming?'

'It's *tomorrow*, darling, *six*. I've done the loveliest chicken thing, you must be *starving*.'

Edward smiled and started upstairs. 'Shan't be long.'

'Gosh, sugar, the *chairs*, and a great big parcel I haven't undone, they're in the living-room.'

Edward returned downstairs and went into the living-room. Sibyl came and stood just behind him, looking past him at the plastic bucket chairs in purple and acid green.

'What on earth are they *for*?'

Edward was silent. How did he know what they were for?

'What's in here, can I open it?'

Edward shrugged. Sibyl tore at the sticky tape holding the parcel until it opened up to reveal the three floor cushions, saffron, magenta and bright blue, a bit squashed from packing.

'How *funny*, darling.'

He knew she had that wary look again.

'They're so completely un-*you*, what on earth got *into* you?'

'Oh, for God's sake forget it!' He turned away and ran upstairs.

CHAPTER XVIII

Going in Friday night Edward saw his rosemary was worse, one green sprig on a dying bush. The mint was worse in its own riotous way. He went into the kitchen.

'Seen the mint?'

'What mint?' She'd nearly finished a salad.

'My mint.'

'Isn't it in the garden?'

'Of course it's in the bloody garden, I mean the way it's taking over.'

'Probably a bit of mutation from old fallouts,' Sibyl said.

Edward smiled. Would she call a meeting about it?

Then she said, 'You say bloody a lot now, darling.'

'Bloody?'

'Why *is* it?'

Edward's voice remained mild. 'Christ, if we're going in for criticizing what about your bloody emphases?'

'What emphases?'

'*Gosh,* don't you *know*?' His mimicry of her high thin voice was bang-on. He smiled as he started from the kitchen.

'Oh, darling,' her voice followed, 'there's a thing hot in the oven and salad made in the fridge, shan't be long if you want to wait for me.'

From the living-room he heard her movements and then the back door, then a little later the station wagon starting. So she'd repented, the meeting was to be elsewhere. No hordes. There'd been no Lumley today, either. If only he'd known there'd be no Lumley instead of straining at every moment, nerves tensed for the phone with Lumley on it. Perhaps it was just Lumley's tactics. The office had shut early so that those who thought it worth while could dolly up. Edward left the building with Miss Gold-man, assuring her he'd be back. He sat in a pub with a whisky. A bilious attack, maybe – something of the sort he'd tell old Strachan on Monday.

Edward got a whisky and took it upstairs to his orderly room. He had a shower and put on old pants and a skivvy; both hung loose now that he'd got so thin. He went down-stairs. The last thing on earth he wanted was Sibyl's thing in the oven. Now or ever. He got a fresh drink, stiffish.

In the living-room he switched on the television and sat down with the morning paper. It was so peaceful he could work on Edward's thing but he might get too engrossed and miss the gardening man. Just as the programme's theme started Sibyl burst in with her shouting mob. Right in the room with him. Edward was aware of the voice starting on thyme, or maybe time it was always short of on the five-minute session. He got up and said quietly in Sibyl's ear, 'Just five minutes – could you take them somewhere else? – he might be speaking of herbs.'

Sibyl's laugh sounded to him strident. '*Darling,* old parsley and stuff, we're trying to save *Mulhaven.*'

Anger rent his head. 'Just five minutes,' he said in the same quiet voice.

Sibyl said, 'I'll get you a book on it, sugar.'

Edward went out to the kitchen. Calling him sugar was a deliberate taunt. He left the kitchen and went out to the garden. He still had his empty glass. He put it down with care, then on impulse began systematically pulling out the mint, roots and all. Then he went on to the rest of his herbs. He could hear their voices. Shouting each other down. On and on in his head. He left the pile of uprooted plants blocking the path and went inside with his glass. He got a fresh drink and went into the living-room. There was no sign anyone noticed him. Edward stood by the

window. Only then he saw the bucket chairs and floor
cushions, extra seats for good old Sibyl's guests. Here Is
My Space by Edward Piper. The television was still going,
the news reader with a pile of disasters they didn't hear.
He watched Wally Jones picking his nose and trying to
interrupt Lionel Ramsay and Max Spenser who were
both talking at once. He watched Sibyl monopolizing
black Brian who seemed roped in on everything now. He'd
have Brian rape Rachel, Lindsay would like that in the
nude. Edward finished his drink and got another. It
didn't stop the stifled feeling. He heard Sibyl's voice: 'He
just *looks* sulky, he isn't really.' Who but himself? He
smiled at Nance who was looking a bit funny. Bloody funny
woman, Nance. Model for serf-woman? He went to the
kitchen and shut himself in. The voices went on. His ability
to shut them out was gone. He wandered round the
table, feeling lost, his hands pressed to his ears. He sat
at the table. He felt without purpose, without identity.
Lumley's voice too he heard, mingled with the others,
asking his stupid baited questions. Even with his hands
deadening sound. He felt no lift from the grog he'd had,
just a bad taste in his mouth.

Hours later he heard Sibyl's voice. 'I said did you eat?'

The bitch could see he hadn't. She set the table round
him, jabbering on about the architectural rarity those pigs
were out to demolish. Would Lindsay stand for this?
Lindsay would say to hell with it. Nothing here to toss
around. No bloody slant scriptwise. Then why did he,
Edward Piper, Writer, put up with it unceasingly?

'Chris'sake, cut the bloody crap.'

'*Edward!*' She was motionless, everything still, a hollow
of silence.

He looked at her through a blur. Sibyl's eyes were
appalled in her stricken face. He didn't want to quarrel. He
wanted it all to be as it was at first. Had it ever been like
that? Hadn't it been false from the start, its falseness

dawning slowly through Sibyl's spaced betraying shocks?

'I just don't want to hear about it, I'm just not interested,' he said in a low voice.

'All right, darling, I understand, it's only, just then — you sounded just like *Lindsay*.'

He didn't know what she was talking about.

'Not just the words, the *voice*.'

Edward stared at her, puzzled. Then he smiled. 'We're both light-headed with hunger, come on, let's eat.'

Sibyl got the thing from the oven, then the salad. They ate in silence. She had the guarded look.

Then Edward said, 'Nice food.'

'That's good, darling, it's rabbit, the poor thing.'

'I can't stand those people around any more,' Edward said.

'It's all over till next year, *really and truly* this time.'

'Not ever. Never again. You tricked me from the start, didn't you?'

'What d'you mean — *tricked*?'

'Everything.' He wanted to say it all: open house, the house itself, the suburban backwater, their marriage, the parents, her earlier marriage. He said, 'Hating my friends —'

'*What* friends?'

'Lindsay. You hated Lindsay.'

'*Lindsay!* Lindsay was *never* your friend.'

Edward took more salad. 'Well,' he said in his calm voice, 'it's going to stop.'

'Oh *Edward*, this all started with *parsley*.'

'Rosemary,' Edward said.

Sibyl giggled. Edward looked at her and he laughed too. Sibyl jumped up and hugged him.

'I'm sorry, darling, I'm always saying I'm sorry, but I *truly* am, *really and truly*, it was just Mul — this urgent thing — I'll get you a whole lot of new herbs to prove how sorry I am.'

Edward patted her hands and she sat down again. 'You ever watched Wally Jones?' he asked. 'Just stands about picking his nose and pulling his little short shirt down trying to get a word in.'

Sibyl laughed so much he thought she'd choke. '*Darling,* that's *priceless,* a *perfect* description.'

Happy Sibyl. Carefree, right from the first. Always the bright side. Worries gone in a flash. He watched her busy with their plates and the coffee things. Buttering him up with brand-new herbs. Until the next careless hurt and laughing recompense. She was still smiling to herself at his description of Wally. Edward wondered how it would be just once to see her face taut with shock, or suspense, and thought it might be rewarding. Not Sibyl, but that face – Rachel, say. Could a person choke to death laughing? Might be good visually. He'd toy around on paper – Edward's thing needed an element of that sort.

Bloody Lumley would be back on his tail Monday. He hadn't fooled Lumley yet.

'We'll go down the coast for Christmas,' he said suddenly.

'Oh, Eddie, *yes,* how *marvellous!*'

'I'll work down there.' Away from Lumley's pressure. 'So long as I'm left in peace.'

She thought he meant the parents. 'They'll understand. They'll just be so thrilled we're *there.*'

'Next Tuesday suit you?'

'Any old time, darling, that's the day before Christmas Eve.'

'Going to board the cats?'

'I told you, I've lined up Nance, she'll feed them and give them a cuddle, they'll be fine.' Sibyl brought their coffee.

'I miss him, Sibyl.'

After a tiny pause she said, 'Lindsay?'

'Yes.'

'Yes.' It had a dubious sound. Then the rush of warmth :

'Poor darling, I'm *sure* you do.'

The warmth was phony, the restraint real. Edward lit a cigarette.

Sibyl said, 'There's something I ought to tell you, it's only fair. I can't bear to hear you keep on – he really was a rat, darling, not the paragon you made him.'

Edward held his breath.

'Diana told me about it, he'd just got a big film to do, the screenplay, it was even in the papers. He was going to rat on you over the other thing.'

Edward had a wild impulse to laugh. He shielded his face with a hand.

'I'm sorry, darling, I know it's a blow, be careful you don't burn your hair. I'm not surprised, I always knew what a slimy opportunist he was.'

Edward said nothing. He was so tired. So tired of Lindsay. He felt a dreadful inertia. Even just to get up and leave the kitchen seemed an effort too big to make. Sibyl gave him more coffee and then began in silence to clear away. She'd said enough, hadn't she? She'd given him something to think about. Was it a trick? Was Sibyl in on it too? This could be a sprat to catch a mackerel: his unwary admission that he knew, an admission of guilt. Was Sibyl as sly as that? Was she so much his enemy?

He dragged himself up from the table, a dead weight. He felt her waiting for his reaction while she pottered about. He moved to the door.

'Of course Diana doesn't call it ratting,' Sibyl said, 'she was really gone on Lindsay.'

He left her to it. Upstairs he locked himself in his room. He didn't sit at his desk because there was no point. His mind was a blank, the typewriter a white elephant. He dropped on the divan, a dead weight.

His hand with the ashtray kept on striking at Lindsay, hammering at Lindsay's skull. Somehow he couldn't stop, couldn't stop the reverberation of blows. He opened his eyes, bewildered to find daylight and himself on the divan and the hammering keeping on.

Then Sibyl's voice: 'Darling, *do* open the door.'

Edward got up and let her in.

'Gosh, I thought—I don't know *what* I thought, it's nearly ten. Some vandal's been at your herbs, darling, they're all pulled out, all that lovely *mint*. What a thing to do.' Then, as it dawned, 'Didn't you even *undress*?'

Edward yawned and turned away. 'You said you'd get me a new lot.'

'But that was because—it wasn't *you*, was it?'

Edward slumped on the side of the divan. He didn't like the feel of Sibyl's unwavering eyes. Why didn't the bitch go?

'It *was* you, I can tell.' She sounded close to tears. 'What a funny thing to do.'

'Can't you leave me in peace for five minutes?' He was at the door as Sibyl retreated before him. She looked scared. He felt like striking out at her because the hammering was still in his head, but at the same time he wanted to cry, to apologize. 'I'm tired, darling, it's been one of those weeks. Think you can cope with the shopping?'

'I did it yesterday,' Sibyl said in a small voice.

'Great.' Edward shut the door. He slumped against it. He couldn't be bothered. It was so simple to let things slide. Just remain silent and every trick they tried would fall flat. Just be his old unassuming, unobtrusive self. Answer their questions but no more, polite but uninformative; go on in his dull little rut. The simplicity of it soothed him. He lay down again and sleep came almost at once.

When he got downstairs around noon he found Sibyl busy outside planting new herbs. She must have gone out specially. He felt a lump in his throat.

'Shan't be long, darling,' she said, 'isn't it lucky the rain's stopped? You must be starving, no breakfast.'

'Shall I finish here?' he asked.

'Okay.' She stood up smiling. 'How's kidneys and bacon sound?'

'Sounds fine.'

Later, doing the dishes, Edward said, 'How's the show coming along?'

Sibyl looked up from a list she was ticking off at the kitchen table. 'Oh, you know – sometimes I think splendidly, then at others I just simply *know* it'll never be ready in time.'

'You'll make it,' Edward said.

Sibyl looked pleased.

The day was heavy passing by. Was it some time in the evening? They were in the living-room. Sibyl was writing on little cards. The plastic bucket chairs and the three floor cushions looked ill-at-ease among Sibyl's chintzy frills. Edward said, 'It's really been hell in the office this week, darling, busy I mean, everyone at once, all the latecomers.'

After a longish pause Sibyl said, 'This is the first year you've missed your office party.'

'I guess it is.'

'When was it?'

'Last night.'

'What about Mr Strachan?'

'What about him?'

'Oh, *you* know, such an old fusspot.'

Edward conquered a wave of anger. Remember it doesn't matter. 'I guess the world won't stop,' he said with a smile.

'Probably not.'

On Sunday Sibyl wrapped Christmas gifts. It took up most of the day.

'D'you think Mummy will like that, I mean *really and truly,* darling?'

'She'll love it, darling, why not?' Edward said with a feeling of clenched teeth, trying to seem interested in the slithery pink thing Sibyl was holding up.

He left her to get on with it and wandered about, unable to do anything. He knew he was waiting for Monday and Lumley. His head was empty, just Sibyl's hissing tissue that followed him all over the house, even out into the garden.

Some time just before dusk in the damp wasteland, Sibyl squealed from the back door. She was waving a newspaper.

'Quick darling, look.'

Edward went towards her with a feeling of dread.

'It's Lindsay's trilogy,' she said, 'they're doing them.'

'They've paid to do them.'

'In yesterday's paper. It says a trilogy of plays by the gifted playwright Lindsay Reid specially written for television, it says the third one was finished by a close colleague – *fancy*, darling, it says Lindsay was murdered in his *prime*, at the very *peak* of his talent.'

Edward smiled and walked past her into the house.

'In February,' Sibyl said following.

'Want a drink?' Edward went into the kitchen.

'*I* know, let's ask Diana to watch them with *us* – here – there's one each Monday for three weeks, she won't feel so awful and *desperate* being here with us.'

'No,' Edward said.

'But darling –'

'No.' He took a glass and the whisky and went up to his room.

He sat at the desk and held his whirling head. It was the wrong move. Already a wrong move. Today he'd discovered he still had Sibyl's trust. How long would he hold it? Bloody Lindsay!

CHAPTER XIX

Not a word from Lumley. All day Monday Edward waited.
He worked hard because it helped the waiting. But it
couldn't make him forget a sudden sprouting of distrust in
the atmosphere around him.

It began with Sibyl. Not speaking all through breakfast,
not a word until he was leaving. 'I just simply don't understand you any more, Edward.' The level voice. She was
really upset.

Then Strachan. Into his office first thing. 'Well, Mr
Piper, what happened on Friday?' Waiting thin and tall for
an explanation.

'A bilious attack, Mr Strachan, I'm sorry, sir, the weather,
I meant to ask my wife to phone but I just felt too ill for
anything. I'm very sorry about it.'

'You're feeling better now?'

'The biliousness, yes. I'm overtired, my wife's very
worried, she's been urging me, we thought we'd join her
parents for Christmas, they're down near Nowra. My wife
thought – is it all right if I finish up today, Mr Strachan?
My wife thinks as soon as possible and hopes we can leave
tomorrow.'

'I agree, Mr Piper, it's best all round, there's talk going
on, you see. Take an extra week, three weeks in all, and
come back your old self. Lately we haven't known you,
you're a different man, you see. That fellow said something
– but of course they must be barking up the wrong tree.'

'Thank you very much, sir.'

'See me before you go, Mr Piper.'

'Of course, sir.'

Even Miss Goldman had a worried look for him now

instead of a smile, although Edward remained as nice to her as ever.

As for Mrs Fleming, the umbrage she'd taken had the look of permanence.

But worse than specific instances was the distrust he could only feel, only guess at.

Yet no Lumley. Edward felt in a way let down, then smiled at himself. No Lumley was great.

Mr Strachan wished him the compliments of the season without the usual handshake. But gave him the usual bonus.

Driving home an enormous sense of relief swamped Edward. No Lumley. Tomorrow they'd be safely away. It wasn't unlikely Lumley had given up. After all, where could he go from here?

Yet Monday turned out to be the worst of days.

Sibyl's station wagon in the road. The usual assortment of neighbours' cars. The sunset glow in the windows. The rain starting again. All three cats mewing in the hall. But no activity or even aroma in the kitchen. And the living-room door shut, that was unprecedented. A sick foreboding turned to panic: Sibyl had left him!

He opened the shut door and heard Lumley's voice, then Sibyl's overriding. 'Darling, that you? Come on in, darling.'

Edward arranged his smile and went in. They couldn't see the thumping of his heart.

Lumley didn't stand up. 'Just a little chat,' he said. He looked dreadfully at home in Sibyl's clutter. He had on a grey raincoat.

Fear churned inside Edward. 'Questions?' he asked politely.

'No, darling,' Sibyl said quickly, too quickly, 'mainly Diana, how long we've known each other, stuff like that.'

Edward lit a cigarette. He sat in the purple bucket chair. Lumley was in the acid green. He had the notebook open. His hat was on the settee.

Lumley said, 'You were just going to tell me, Mrs Piper,

what time your husband got home that night.'

'You didn't say which night,' Sibyl said in her motion-opposing voice.

'The night Mr Reid met his death, Tuesday, December 9th.' He watched her little play of trying to recall. 'Mr Piper is vague about it,' he added.

'Gosh, we're *both* vague about things like that,' Sibyl said with a false laugh. 'I don't *time* him, I'm not a *clock-watcher*, he knows I'm often out and I know he's often late. He works beyond the call of duty.'

'But there are some nights you expect him at a fixed time?'

'*Some* nights, yes, if anything's *planned*, but then I may be suddenly out when Edward gets home and he's very forbearing about it.'

'But that night?' Lumley insisted.

Sibyl darted a look at Edward. She'd see the tension in his face, in his whole body. He felt stuck to the bucket chair.

'I simply can't remember,' Sibyl said, 'maybe a *tiny* bit later than usual but it could have been traffic and rain,' her voice seemed to crack and she rushed on, 'but if you're thinking what I think you are you're *crazy* – why, Edward's the lambiest thing on two legs.' She finished in a sort of incredulous shriek.

Lumley nodded, unimpressed. He jotted something in the notebook then smiled at Edward. 'I'd like a word with Mrs Piper alone.'

Edward felt rigid all over as he stood up. The worst of days, because it had drawn in Sibyl.

'Go and have a drink, darling,' Sibyl said gaily. She was doing her best to disguise the torment of his stiff steps to the door. Dear darling Sibyl.

Outside in the hall he stood stockstill a moment. There seemed no point in any direction, in movement of any kind. Then out of the blue he remembered Lindsay's old scripts.

He ran upstairs.

The scripts were on his desk. Then it occurred to him: why not? If he did away with them mightn't it look worse? Diana, who knew everything, would know about the scripts Lindsay had tossed at him. He sank in the chair at his desk.

And despite any lie Diana had told Lumley, Lindsay's new commission didn't necessarily mean he'd scotched the ecology film. Lindsay had been dead keen from the start. Behind the critical banter there'd been a real sense of purpose for Lindsay in the ecology thing. There'd been times they'd seen eye to eye, times Lindsay had said, 'Sounds great, old boy.'

Without warning a terrible remorse engulfed him. He clung to the desk as the only solid. He let his head fall down on his arms.

Edward runs at Lindsay and grips his throat. Brian steps in and grabs Edward's arm, verbal remonstrance. Edward renews attack, they struggle. Rachel is weeping on a floor cushion, comforted by Edward's son. Edward sees the danger almost succumbed to. Let bloody Lindsay go scot-free and meet his own damnation in his own —

The knocking grew insistent. Edward got up and opened the door. 'Come on in, old boy,' he said to Lumley, 'take a pew.'

Lumley smiled and came in but remained standing. 'You borrowed scripts from Mr Reid.' His eyes were on them. His hat was on.

Edward's eyes followed Lumley's. He cursed the feeling of guilt that must show in his face. 'Yes.'

'You still have them?'

'Of course. I can't very well return them, can I? Not exactly borrowed – he wanted my views, he was a bit worried about his style.'

'I see. And he didn't ask for them back when he called off the film?'

'If he called off the film he didn't tell me about it.'

'Miss Lucas insists that you knew.'

'You've her word against mine.'

'Yes,' Lumley said. The mild tone was neutral but Edward knew better.

'I suppose Miss Lucas told you about the scripts,' he said.

'Your wife happened to mention them.' Lumley sat on Edward's divan. It made Edward's flesh creep. Lumley got out his precious notebook. 'Mr Reid brought you a tie from Hayman Island.'

'Yes, I told you, here –' Edward went to the unit and showed Lumley the tie hanging among his own. 'Not my taste, but he meant well. I suppose I'm being sentimental in keeping it.'

'And when did he give it to you?'

Edward shrugged. Lumley's question sounded like a trap. 'I didn't make a note of the date.'

'I see. Last Thursday you told me he gave it to you on the Monday, the day before he was murdered, while the two of you were having drinks at a number of hotels.'

Edward put a hand to his head. If only he could remember, if only he had a notebook like Lumley's, if only Lindsay would walk through the door with his 'Sorry, old boy'.

'He paid back some money he owed you at the same time – does that help you remember?'

'That must be right.' Edward went to the window. The desolation outside looked worse than ever but it was better than Lumley.

'Miss Lucas says the tie was still there that night, the Monday night, in Mr Reid's flat, still wrapped in its tissue paper, I think pink, I believe Miss Lucas said pink – yes. They spoke of it together.'

Christ! Edward turned. He said firmly, 'Miss Lucas is mistaken.'

'I see.' Lumley settled himself more comfortably on Edward's divan. 'We'll see.' He riffled the pages of his notebook.

A new thought occurred to Edward to terrify him : that Diana knew for certain he was Lindsay's visitor on the evening Lindsay died. In that case Diana believed it was Edward's doing, and all this wasn't motivated just by malice as he'd thought. And if she knew, Lumley knew too. They were playing with him. At once he knew this to be absurd. If Lumley knew that, Edward would be in a cell. He was free, so Lumley didn't know. He was safe.

Lumley looked up with a smile. 'Did you know Miss Lucas warned your wife against you right from the first?'

Rage rose in Edward. 'I'm not surprised.'

'Why should she?'

'I told you, an instant prejudice.'

'Miss Lucas describes you as a solitary man, although not from choice, she believes.'

'Miss Lucas is the fount of all wisdom.'

'You sleep in here?' Lumley looked around Edward's room as if just seeing it.

'Sometimes. If it has any bearing on anything.'

'This is where you write?'

'Yes.' Edward ground it out.

'You said at our meeting on December 17th that your wife had stiff competition in landing you, a great old chase, you said.'

Edward slumped in the desk chair. All the bloody crap.

'Miss Lucas has a different story,' Lumley said.

Edward looked across at Lumley, puzzled as to his purpose. 'Does it matter?'

'Just inconsistencies, Mr Piper. Perhaps they don't matter until the truth is required. Then they're seen as lies.' The gentleness was gone from Lumley's voice. 'For instance, this room, you've made a very nice job of it, quite different from the rest of the house. It must have taken some planning, but you needed it to do your writing.'

Edward twisted his hands together then got out a cigarette so he'd stop. He said nothing.

'Your wife says you don't write.'

'Professional jealousy.'

Lumley smiled as if Edward had made a joke. 'You know that's not true, don't you? Your wife loves you very much. She wishes you did write instead of manufacturing excuses for not doing so.'

'I want a drink,' Edward said. He went to the door, crushing the cigarette in his fist.

Lumley was there too and took Edward's arm. 'I'll leave now, Mr Piper, just think things over after I'm gone.'

Edward laughed. 'You crazy bastard.'

Lumley opened the door and turned with a direct look. 'There was blood on his forehead, not much, he'd been struck with force, in all probability with the ashtray, a very heavy square piece of glass, nasty weapon. It was quite clean, of course. Good evening, Mr Piper, I'll see myself down.'

Edward sat at the desk. He had no sense of time or even of place. Only Lindsay's time, Lindsay's place, seated at Lindsay's desk in the straight-backed chair with the orange seat and the drink Lindsay gave him he didn't touch except to pour it down Lindsay's sink and Lindsay saying '... might as well call a halt – you wouldn't stand a chance – you lack the knack – the so-called partnership's over – an envious little toad, Piper – say it was just a tease – your hangdog bloody envy . . .' engraved for all time, all of it, all the betrayal, for ever on his brain. And the heavy green glass ashtray.

Suddenly he laughed. If Lindsay had been using a different ashtray, something lightweight, he'd be alive now, looking forward to the screening of his trilogy, work begun on his new commission. Diana would be the nothing she'd always been, Sibyl her old happy trusting self, no Lumley, no torment, no circle closing to stifle him inside it with his guilt. Guilt for no crime, just an accident. All because of an ashtray. Edward sobbed on the desk.

'Darling, darling, don't, it breaks my heart.' Hands lifted his head, arms went round him, cradled him in their thinness.

He couldn't look at her face where love of late was full of doubts and tenderness had no substance. 'Darling,' she said, 'come downstairs.'

He knew she'd stick by him. His Sibyl, bless her, his Rachel. Everything would be all right with Sibyl.

'Mr Lumley's worried about you, darling.'

Edward laughed.

'Darling, please – *don't*. That's the sort of thing – you're all mixed-up, darling, people have noticed. Mr Lumley thinks you're rejecting the truth, that Lindsay's dead he means, he's seen it before, he says – not *purposely,* just that you've got things *twisted* like they can be in a dream – he says it's a sort of crisscross.'

Crisscross, Edward thought. Something in that as a title? Crisscrossing relationships between organisms and their environments, between himself and Lindsay.

'Darling, there's nothing to *smile* about – gosh, what's there *funny* about all this?'

Edward clung to Sibyl. Why did he strangle the sob? It wasn't unmanly to cry, was it? Men had tear ducts too. They had emotions. Fear and terror. Manly, womanly: idiotic unreal words.

'Have a good cry, darling,' Sibyl crooned, cradling his head again. 'It's all the terrible pressure.'

Christ, if she bloody knew. Lindsay, Lumley, Diana. Guilt.

'I'm sure he doesn't think it was *you*,' Sibyl said, '*nobody* does, how *could* they?'

Edward went stiff. Too many emphases. 'That bitch

Diana,' he said.

'But darling, Diana doesn't come into this at *all* – how does Diana come in?'

What new trick was Sibyl up to? Long talks they'd had behind his back. Telling Lumley he had Lindsay's scripts. Edward pushed her away and stood up. 'I need a bloody whisky.'

Sibyl edged back, staring. 'It's that,' she said, 'that's just what he meant, like two quite different people.'

Christ, what was she on about now?

'I told him it's just being so upset because Lindsay was your best friend. I said grief often makes people funny and all you needed was a good long rest.' She was at the door now, the open door that let them all come in. 'Just think, darling, this time tomorrow we'll be down the coast and you can relax and forget all about it and sleep for hours on end.'

Sibyl. Edward went to her and held her close. Thank God for Sibyl.

'Come downstairs,' she said, 'it's this room.'

They went downstairs. 'Scotch filet, zucchini and mushrooms,' Sibyl said, 'Sounds good?'

Edward smiled. In the kitchen Sibyl got him a gin and tonic.

'You told him we were going away?'

'Well yes, darling, I did. He thought it the best thing you could do.'

'That's good.' Edward kept his smile. But he knew this could be a new kind of Lumley trick. He didn't trust Lumley one little bit.

Late that night, when his packing was done and he knew Sibyl was asleep, he took Lindsay's two scripts and poked them down among the rubbish in the big garbage bin in the garden. They weren't proof of anything but he felt better with them gone. They'd be gone for good when Nance and Jeff put the bin out for the garbage men.

CHAPTER XX

Nance and Jeff waved them off in the rain. Umbrellas, galoshes, fatuities. Sibyl waved to the two cats wishing them ill from the open back door. The third would be already off in a huff.

'Hope the weather clears up for you.'

'For everyone,' Sibyl laughed.

'Don't worry about the cats.'

'Thanks, Nance.'

'Hope you land some whoppers,' Nance said.

Sibyl laughed. 'We're going to *sleep,* not fish.'

'Love to your parents.'

Jeff smiled at Edward. 'Be there for lunch?'

'Ask Rachel, she's the driver.'

'Rachel?'

He caught Sibyl's worried look. 'New pet name,' he said with a grin. 'Let's go, darling.'

They were in Sibyl's station wagon. She started up. The last goodbyes and Merry Christmases.

It was good to be going, after all. The parents weren't Lumley. He'd left Lumley behind. Edward relaxed as the distance grew behind them. This was the old reality back, the life he'd thought so dull it must be escaped from. He leaned towards Sibyl and kissed her cheek. 'Merry Christmas, darling.'

'Oh, Eddie, isn't it *lovely* to get away.'

Even Eddie lost its sting. 'Let me know when you're tired and I'll take over.'

'I'm fine, darling, you relax.'

They stopped in Kiama for coffee and got to Nowra before twelve. Stretches of road were under water. Sibyl turned on to the dirt road that led to the parents' place.

Luckily it rose, but even so its surface was badly eroded by the rain. The rain came down in buckets. The parents' place was built on the ranch house principle, but hollyhocks, a picket fence and frilly curtains imbued a cottagey look. Sibyl pulled up and tooted. Daddy appeared round the side of the house in gumboots, mac and sou'wester and waved Sibyl into the garage. Mummy was in the front door with clasped hands and her pointy nose already red with excitement.

'How's my girl?' Daddy enveloped Sibyl in a wet hug, then clapped Edward's shoulder. 'They're sandbagging the river banks today, that's how bad it is, I'll get back down to lend a hand after lunch.'

Kisses all round. Lunch a baked macaroni seafood thing. Sibyl's radiance. Daddy on the flood danger, now extreme: the river swollen with previous rains and floodwaters from inland downpours. Mummy edging in an occasional word about aired sheets, a good rest and Christmas dinner. Edward listened without listening. He felt rested; he felt, after all, safe here. He let Mummy give him a second helping and smiled when she gave his arm a loving squeeze.

'You'll want to get settled in,' Daddy told them undeniably. 'Then dinner tonight with us, you don't want to disappoint Rosemary, then tomorrow's your own in your own little place, how's that?'

'Lovely, darlings,' Sibyl said and Edward went on smiling.

'Then over here Christmas morning,' Rosemary said.

'Lovely,' Edward said.

The holiday shack he'd dreaded as a rickety structure silvered by salt spray turned out to be solidly brick, clean and comfortably furnished. Hadn't Sibyl said fibro? It was close to the parents' place, over the road fifty yards along, on a knoll. Edward liked the nearness he should have hated. He was amused at himself.

'*Darling*, isn't it *marvellous*?' Sibyl cried.

'It's great.'

'*Look,* Mummy's thought of *everything.*' Sibyl was rushing about peering in drawers and cupboards.

'In here, too,' Edward said, 'come and see.'

Sibyl rushed into the bedroom. 'Oh, Edward!'

The double bed shone with a turquoise satin quilt, shirred and flounced, with turquoise plastic reading lamps to match mounted on the wall. A bedside table on each side held identical cut-glass vases of flowers.

'The darlings,' Sibyl said chokily. 'That's her best bedspread she's lent us till the patchwork's done.'

Edward hugged her. They kissed. They were very close.

'Poor Daddy sandbagging in this downpour, all ablebodied men, women too,' Sibyl said.

Edward stroked her chestnut hair.

They unpacked and settled in. Edward cleaned Mummy's hands from the kitchen and then made afternoon tea. Mummy had thought of everything: groceries, milk, everything.

Sibyl was first in bed, not smoking, smiling, wide open eyes. Edward went to the bathroom. He'd thought a safe backwater, but now under the shower he thought exultantly why not the mainstream? Lumley would never have relinquished him if he'd had anything to go on. Edward was suddenly convinced his trial was over. Perhaps Sibyl knew, Lumley could have told her it was one of those baffling cases where even the unlikeliest leads must be systematically followed. Hopeless, infuriating to those caught up, but obligatory to the system. It would explain Sibyl's happiness. Waiting for him in the double bed with her eyes open, not smoking.

He thought of dinner with the parents set in their ways. Seasoned roast veal and Daddy's sandbags saga. Edward had succumbed uncritically to both.

It was nice in a double bed, together. Sibyl's arms enfolded him. The rain lashing outside made it all the cosier. Sibyl caressed him, he responded with ardour.

But it was no good. The auguries weren't enough after all. He was no longer a man, Lindsay had seen to that. And Lumley. He was Lumley's quarry.

'Never mind, darling, after a few days' rest, just don't *worry*, darling.'

In the morning he kept his depression hidden. They had breakfast and shared the washing-up. The rain had eased and a lightening here and there in the black cloud pall hinted at a turning-point.

'Any plans in particular, darling?' Edward asked.

'I thought perhaps –'

Daddy's voice came in along with Daddy in the same rain togs. 'What time's your friend arriving, dear?'

'Oh, about midday.'

Friend?

'Sleep well, son?'

'Thanks, very well.' Friend? 'More sandbags?'

'Done all we can. Only prayer can save us now. These two days'll be the test, level's rising, expecting the peak at any time. Plenty of outlying farms isolated days ago. Thanks, dear,' he took one of Sibyl's cigarettes. 'Well, if you feel like it I'm to tell you there's cold veal for lunch, but only if you feel like it.' He moved to the door. 'We haven't seen Diana for quite a while, still the same nice little girl?'

Edward stopped listening. He went to the bathroom. The door had a bolt. His rage was all for Sibyl. But the wild black moment had gone. If they'd been alone with a weapon to hand – but circumstances had saved them both. Edward leaned against the wall. He felt exhausted, as if he'd come in from a violent storm. But the rage against Sibyl churned on inside. Diana coming, arranged by Sibyl who hadn't told him. This wasn't forgetfulness, it was a deliberate conspiring with Lumley. Lumley's new trick. They'd hatched it together among Sibyl's frills. They thought a confrontation by Diana would break him.

'Darling, you in there?'

'Half a second.' So she was going to do her innocence act.
'*Do* hurry, darling, I'm *bursting*, three cups of tea.'

Edward took a deep breath. He looked at his hands. The shaking had almost stopped. He slid back the bolt. Sibyl rushed past him in a frenzy and slammed the door.

He went to the bedroom and got his cigarettes out. The first cigarette since leaving Sydney. He heard the rush of water, the door, then Sibyl coming. He turned smiling.

'Don't tell me, let me guess: you forgot.'

'Forgot what?'

'Diana.'

'I told you, darling, I'm sure – I bet you just weren't *listening*, you know what you're like when I ramble on and on. She's sleeping at their place, she won't foist herself on you – *us* – if we don't feel like it. I feel so terribly *sorry* for her. It really was a lasting thing they had going.'

'I see.' A Lumley expression denoting disbelief.

'I hope you do, darling. *Please* be nice to her.'

Edward was, in a neutral way. Diana came, thinner than ever, just before noon. She kissed them all but Edward, but then they scarcely knew each other. But she smiled at him, didn't exclude him, there was no special significance, no withdrawal, in her manner towards him. They all sat down round the cold veal and a cheap sweet Sauternes-type. Perhaps Diana's animus against him had run itself out. It was Sibyl he hated for the visit, not Diana. Sibyl had fixed it.

He escaped when lunch was over. It was easy. He didn't count. They hardly noticed. It was the same with Sibyl's people at home in Fernydale. The rain had eased, almost stopped. Edward sat on the verandah of his new holiday home and stared at the puddles in the road.

'We're going for a swim, coming?' Sibyl with Diana.

'Too lazy.'

'Do you good.'

'Can't be bothered, some other time.'

They went off together in Sibyl's station wagon.

It was true he couldn't be bothered. He'd lost interest. He had no energy, no purpose. He thought, I just don't care any more. Everyone but himself was agog with the floods. Why should he care? What did it matter if people drowned in floods? If the right people drowned. He'd like Sibyl to vanish, just vanish without any move on his part. Drown somehow. At the same time he'd be lost without her. If Sibyl would somehow vanish he'd sell the house. No doubt that bossy mean old limping bastard would want a say in that, more than a say, all the say. The house should be in both their names, he should have been firm at the time. Taken a stand on everything. Had they ever talked about wills? It was such an effort to think. He was tired of manoeuvring. Perhaps Lumley would vanish too. It would be great if Lumley somehow dropped off his tail. Then he and Lindsay could finish the film and go on to more and better. Scriptwise, they were bloody well-matched: Edward's ideas and Lindsay's know-how. High time he heard from Lindsay again.

Green and yellow stripes. The deck chair he was in. It came as a shock. Verandah of a strange house, Sibyl's, in a wet landscape dotted with dwellings among rain-beaten trees. Lindsay was dead. He'd been in a muddle again.

He went inside. What to do? He should have gone with the girls, his old amenable self. He walked across to the parents' place. Mummy was alone, fiddling around as usual, busy bee.

'Anything you'd like doing?' Edward asked.

'Oh, didn't you go for a swim, dear?' Mummy never left the obvious unsaid.

'Wish I had, I'll go next time. Anything you want done?'

'Well, dear, there's the rubbish for the tip but you won't feel like that, I'm not even going to ask you.'

'I'd like to.'

'Well, that *is* kind. Tom's so much in demand in these bad days. You can take the ute.'

Under Mummy's direction Edward placed cartons and bags of tins and bottles in the back of the utility van. Then Mummy told him how to get there.

Edward drove round the knoll their holiday house was on and felt the ocean smell full in his face. The road was wilder here but the tip was not far along on the right of the road. A stationary car was on the left, on the ocean side. Another rubbish tipper. Edward pulled up on a ribbon of tussocky grass on the right. He got out and hauled the first of the cartons down. The tip wasn't far off the road, through trees. Edward emptied the carton and started back with it.

Coming out of the trees he saw Lumley. Lumley was unobtrusive by the stationary car, his back to Edward, pretending to look at the view which was hazy with broken clouds. But Edward saw him, Edward who knew Lumley's shape indelibly. The strange thing was he felt no panic. What did Lumley want? Just watching to see Edward didn't make a dash for it? Edward had an impulse to go over and say hello, but Lumley got in his car as though unaware of Edward.

Lumley could never prove anything. What was his game? He didn't know Edward's lifelong training in fortitude. Seeing Lumley made Edward want to live. The feeling was urgent. He had to outwit Lumley. Lumley's car didn't start. Lumley was a patient man. Edward went over to the car.

'Holiday?'

'Something of the sort.' Lumley smiled. 'You look rested.'

'Shouldn't I?' Edward smiled too. He felt himself a match for Lumley. 'Staying somewhere nice, on safe high ground?'

'Thank you, yes. The sea looks angry.' Lumley's glasses

shone when his head moved.

'They're mucking it up, no wonder it's angry,' Edward said.

'I wouldn't worry about it, Mr Piper.' Lumley's voice was consoling. Lumley was a fool.

'Don't you care? They spill oil in it, dump poisons in it, they're messing up everything.'

'No point upsetting yourself, Mr Piper.'

If Lumley were indicative of mass intelligence, maybe even a cut above, then there was certainly no point in worrying. So no point in Edward's film. An audience of Lumleys gave the film no meaning. No worries, Lumley said. Lumley didn't care about the earth's ruin, all his petty concentration was narrowed on Edward. And Edward needed his own concentration, every single moment of it, for thwarting Lumley. He'd known a long time, deep inside himself, that the film was lost, ever since Lindsay's dying. He'd clung to a myth. So scrap it. Go on as before, before it all started, before Lindsay started the agonizing mess by pretending to seek Edward's help. Before had attractions he'd never appreciated, never even noticed. Stability, Sibyl's love, comfort, respect, a job he liked and was good at. The film was dead, bury it. He wanted to live, live as before, make it up to Sibyl.

'I'd better finish my chores,' Edward said. He smiled at Lumley. 'See you around.'

'I expect so.'

'Merry Christmas.'

Lumley's car was still there when Edward came back after emptying the last of the rubbish. Edward got in the utility, drove on a short distance, then turned and without a glance at Lumley drove back to the parents' house. He'd won that round, possibly the most important round of all. Lumley had wanted fear from him.

CHAPTER XXI

Christmas morning was like all Christmas mornings. Squeals and kisses and headaches threatening. Diana had presents for everyone, even for Edward: something soft in pink tissue paper. Edward put it aside. Sibyl gave him a brief-case and a purple silk dressing-gown. 'For your new personality,' she laughed. Daddy took bossy charge of everything, even to the opening of gifts.

'What's this?' He snatched up the pink tissue. 'It's yours, son, like me to open it for you?'

'I can manage, thanks.' He was ready now. He knew what was inside. He unwrapped the tissue and let the bright blue tie fall out with the hateful bare pink girl facing them all. 'Thanks, Diana, lovely taste.' He saw Sibyl clap her hands, laughing at the joke of it. They must have got a job lot on Hayman Island, fun things for Lindsay's cronies.

Breakfast was noisy and piecemeal. With the river expected to peak today any sense of Christmas peace, fugitive enough, was shattered. Mummy and Diana got ready for church. Daddy was off to order back the waters. Mummy thought Sibyl and Edward should go to church too. Sibyl glanced at Edward and told Mummy no.

When they'd gone Edward took some aspirin. 'I'm going for a walk,' he said.

'All right, darling, you need it, you know, you *never* exercise now, you used to be so beautifully *muscley*.' She took his arm.

'You coming?'

'Of *course* I'm coming, I won't let you drown without *me*.'

There were patches of blue sky. The humidity needed a

wind to shift it. They held hands.

Lumley would be watching their house, both houses. No doubt he'd talked to the parents, who would fall over themselves to build his case against Edward. He'd have secret meetings with Diana. And Sibyl?

On the way Sibyl said, 'There's talk of stacking more sandbags along the most vulnerable parts of the river.'

'You scared?'

'No, silly, I'm just so sorry for flooded farmers. I just hope no one's caught if anything happens. The level's still rising, Daddy says, he's sure it'll peak today.'

Edward's eyes found the little church and in it he saw the symbol of everything that had gone wrong. Even there Lindsay had let him down. The church was on a rise.

'Let's go over there,' he said.

'Where?'

'Our little church, a sentimental visit.'

'Well —' Sibyl paused, 'there's no service on because it's such low ground in between.'

'You *are* scared.'

'Of *course* I'm not, besides, everyone's alerted.'

His arm round her, just like lovers.

'Oh, I'm *so* glad we came, aren't you, darling, after all?'

Edward smiled and gave her a squeeze.

The church had the same musty smell, the same fresh floral arrangements, dying, done by Mummy and her committee of women, taking turns. The same ugly modern stained-glass windows. The same depressing old drapes and sticky pews. Hate churned in Edward.

'Darling?' Sibyl's voice close behind him, small, hesitant. 'Diana says you went to see Lindsay that night.'

He turned smiling to face her. 'Which night?'

'The night he was — he died.'

'I didn't,' Edward said in his quiet voice. 'It's a matter of who you believe, isn't it?'

'You of course, but it's just that Lindsay told her–'

'And *you* believe Lindsay?' His smile felt crooked.

'But Diana–'

'Diana hates me, you know that.'

'Yes, but–'

'I don't want to talk about it, Sibyl, I'm sick of the subject of Lindsay.'

'All right, darling.'

They poked around the church, their closeness gone. He saw her anxious face. What else had she been going to say?

Sibyl was first to see it from the doorway. 'Edward! Gosh! Look!'

Floodwater filling the low land had almost reached the church itself. The path from the gate was already covered by water swelling with vindictive speed towards the base of the three steps below the little porch.

'It must have broken all the way along,' Sibyl said in a frightened voice.

The danger Edward saw wasn't from flooding. 'Yes but what?' he said.

Sibyl turned, puzzled.

'You were going to say something else about Diana.'

'She told that man, Mr Lumley–oh, Edward, look, it's covered the first step.' She was terrified.

Oh Edward! he mimicked her, but it was in his head with satisfying exaggeration. Sibyl tried to smile, tried to be brave. Couldn't she see they were in no danger? Edward gripped her arms. She let him, grateful, then saw his expression.

'*Edward!*' The smile drained from her face. '*Edward!*' she squeaked.

'*Edward!*' he mocked.

She struggled, panic making her almost a match for him. Finally he had to hold her down on the floor of the church with his hand over her mouth so they wouldn't be seen and saved by rescuers looking for strays. She went on struggling. Edward's physical strength came into its own again.

Sibyl's pale blue eyes had a wild look.

Did he want her to give him a reason for living? Did he want to do this? The enormity of it struck him. He snatched the hand from over her mouth. 'Sibyl – darling – ' a sob choked in his throat.

'It's all right, darling, you don't feel well, you're not well, you're so thin, I shouldn't have told you but it's all right, you didn't, you *couldn't* – ' Sibyl's voice sounded strangled – 'darling, *please* sugar, we've got to *do* something.'

His grip went back tighter than before. He wanted the flood to come up and fill the church. He wanted to drown too; have done. Have the water win out. The world was better to die in than to live in. No such luck. They'd said it would peak today and it had, now it would fall. He'd meant to save Sibyl. He hadn't wanted her dead, or Lindsay. He'd been trying to rescue Sibyl, hadn't he? They'd see that, wouldn't they? Even Lumley. Lumley must grant him that. He couldn't see through the tears. Sibyl was all he had. Lumley would see.

He stood in the doorway. Lumley *could* see, now, this minute, they were almost here. A launch, somebody waving. Rescuers, Daddy among them in his sou'wester.

'Thank God!' Sibyl leaned against the little porch as if spent.

He'd thought – dear God! He moved to her. Gratitude stuck the words of love in his throat. Sibyl flinched from him, fear in her eyes. Distrust. Love for ever gone.

The sun came out. Lumley's glasses glinted.